Vengeance Delayed

"Now wait just a damn minute!" the sheriff cried. "Mr. Palmer and his friends are prepared to sign..."

"The hell with what they're prepared to sign!" Clint stormed. "It was murder."

The sheriff began to sweat profusely. "Be reasonable, Clint! You know that you can outdraw this man! Why, you'd be doing the same thing he did to old Ed! Two wrongs don't make a right. And you were a lawman too many years not to see the truth of what I'm saying."

Clint expelled a deep breath. The sheriff was right. Two wrongs didn't make a right. But a good old man who had probably had a little too much to drink was dead for no better reason than that he'd been proud of a beautiful leather holster.

Clint took a step back. "You and me," he said in a low, hard tone of voice. "There will come a day."

Palmer forced a stiff grin. "I guess there will. But *I'll* choose the time and the circumstances, not you. A smart gambler never bucks the odds."

"You already have," Clint said as he turned on his heel and stomped out of the sheriff's office.

Also in THE GUNSMITH series

MACKLIN'S WOMEN
THE CHINESE GUNMAN
BULLETS AND BALLOTS
THE RIVERBOAT GANG
KILLER GRIZZLY
NORTH OF THE BORDER
EAGLE'S GAP
CHINATOWN HELL
THE PANHANDLE SEARCH
WILDCAT ROUNDUP
THE PONDEROSA WAR
TROUBLE RIDES A FAST HORSE
DYNAMITE JUSTICE
THE POSSE
NIGHT OF THE GILA
THE BOUNTY WOMEN
WILD BILL'S GHOST
THE MINER'S SHOWDOWN
ARCHER'S REVENGE
SHOWDOWN IN RATON
WHEN LEGENDS MEET
DESERT HELL
THE DIAMOND GUN
DENVER DUO
HELL ON WHEELS
THE LEGEND MAKER
WALKING DEAD MAN
CROSSFIRE MOUNTAIN
THE DEADLY HEALER
THE TRAIL DRIVE WAR
GERONIMO'S TRAIL
THE COMSTOCK GOLD FRAUD
TEXAS TRACKDOWN
THE FAST DRAW LEAGUE
SHOWDOWN IN RIO MALO
OUTLAW TRAIL
HOMESTEADER GUNS
FIVE CARD DEATH
TRAILDRIVE TO MONTANA
TRIAL BY FIRE
THE OLD WHISTLER GANG
DAUGHTER OF GOLD
APACHE GOLD
PLAINS MURDER

DEADLY MEMORIES
THE NEVADA TIMBER WAR
NEW MEXICO SHOWDOWN
BARBED WIRE AND BULLETS
DEATH EXPRESS
WHEN LEGENDS DIE
SIX-GUN JUSTICE
MUSTANG HUNTERS
TEXAS RANSOM
VENGEANCE TOWN
WINNER TAKE ALL
MESSAGE FROM A DEAD MAN
RIDE FOR VENGEANCE
THE TAKERSVILLE SHOOT
BLOOD ON THE LAND
SIX-GUN SIDESHOW
MISSISSIPPI MASSACRE
THE ARIZONA TRIANGLE
BROTHERS OF THE GUN
THE STAGECOACH THIEVES
JUDGMENT AT FIRECREEK
DEAD MAN'S JURY
HANDS OF THE STRANGLER
NEVADA DEATH TRAP
WAGON TRAIN TO HELL
RIDE FOR REVENGE
DEAD RINGER
TRAIL OF THE ASSASSIN
SHOOT-OUT AT CROSSFORK
BUCKSKIN'S TRAIL
HELLDORADO
THE HANGING JUDGE
THE BOUNTY HUNTER
TOMBSTONE AT LITTLE HORN
KILLER'S RACE
WYOMING RANGE WAR
GRAND CANYON GOLD
GUNS DON'T ARGUE
GUNDOWN
FRONTIER JUSTICE
GAME OF DEATH
THE OREGON STRANGLER
BLOOD BROTHERS
ARIZONA AMBUSH
THE VENGEANCE TRAIL

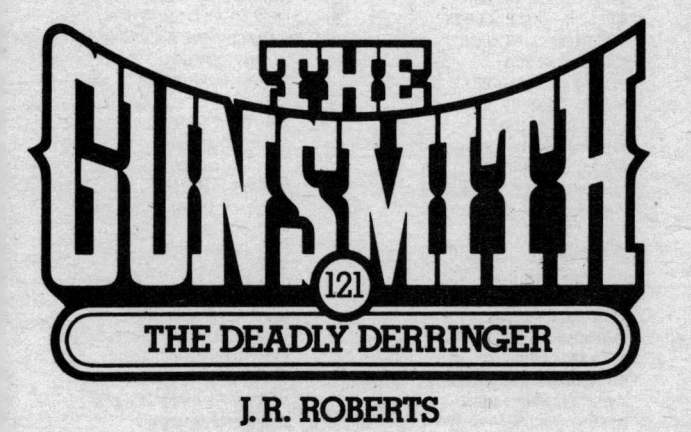

THE Gunsmith
121
THE DEADLY DERRINGER

J. R. ROBERTS

JOVE BOOKS, NEW YORK

THE DEADLY DERRINGER

A Jove Book / published by arrangement with
the author

PRINTING HISTORY
Jove edition / January 1992

All rights reserved.
Copyright © 1992 by Robert J. Randisi.
This book may not be reproduced in whole or in part,
by mimeograph or any other means, without permission.
For information address: The Berkley Publishing Group,
200 Madison Avenue, New York, New York 10016.

ISBN: 0-515-10755-7

Jove Books are published by The Berkley Publishing Group,
200 Madison Avenue, New York, New York 10016.
The name "JOVE" and the "J" logo
are trademarks belonging to Jove Publications, Inc.

PRINTED IN THE UNITED STATES OF AMERICA

10 9 8 7 6 5 4 3 2 1

ONE

Clint Adams didn't know why he'd decided to spend a few months in the southwestern Nevada mining town of Candelaria. Candelaria meant "Candle Mass" in Spanish, but this was one of the most godless mining towns that Clint had ever visited. The town was located out in the sun-blasted hills not so far northeast of Death Valley. And although Candelaria was almost two years old, a man could count its trees on the fingers of one hand because water had to be freighted into town and sold for a nickel a gallon. A bath cost two dollars and, even at those prices, the water tasted of alkali and would kill trees, not to mention destroying the insides of a man.

But the ore and money were flowing in Candelaria and Clint Adams was raking it in along with everyone else. He was the only decent gunsmith for perhaps fifty miles around and when he'd repaired every weapon in this mining district, Clint figured he'd move on with a good stake before the real heat of summer turned Candelaria into a hell's kitchen.

Even now, in early May, the temperature was rising into the upper eighties. And to make matters worse, in the afternoons a hot wind blew a fine, powdery dust through town. The dust would infiltrate everything. It would sift under doors and work its way into the very creases of a man's flesh so that he would get raw in the joints if he didn't bath quite regularly.

No doubt about it, Clint thought as he finished up working on a rifle and prepared to close up the little shop he'd rented, Candelaria was a hard, dirty mining town. Mining accidents were commonplace and rarely did a week pass that at least one or two men were not gunned down in some saloon brawl or murdered for their wages.

The door opened and a grizzled old miner shuffled inside. "You closed yet?"

"In about five minutes. Your Colt .45 is ready, Ed."

Ed's eyes narrowed a little. He was a man in his midfifties, rough and humped in the shoulders. His hands were thick and knobby from years of hard work and his movements gave every impression of a man who had worked too hard for too long.

"How much is your damage?"

"Not too much," Clint said as he reached under his workbench and retrieved the man's scarred old Colt pistol. "I had to replace a spring in the trigger mechanism and give it a good cleaning and oiling. There are some parts that are getting pretty worn, but you said to leave be anything that doesn't need fixing."

"That's right." Ed grunted as he took his sixgun and turned it one way and then the other in his hands. He cocked back the hammer, aimed at the ceiling and pulled the trigger. The hammer fell harmlessly on an empty cylinder.

"You shouldn't do that," Clint said. "It'll damage the gun."

But Ed didn't seem to care. "How much?"

"Three dollars and fifty cents," Clint said. "And I'd advise you to buy some fresh bullets. Those that were

THE DEADLY DERRINGER

in your gun looked to have been there for quite some time. Old ammunition can get you in serious trouble by either firing when you don't expect, or not firing when you are in trouble and can't afford to have something go wrong."

"Hell." Ed grunted, pulling money out of his pants pocket. "I don't find the need to shoot this damn thing more than once or twice a year. And as for ammunition, well, I'll wait until get up to Carson City again. I can save fifty cents or a dollar a box."

"That's your choice," Clint said, "but wearing a gun loaded with faulty ammunition is worse than wearing no gun at all. It's that dangerous."

"Then I'll take six new bullets," Ed told him.

Clint shook his head but he did load fresh ammunition in the repaired gun. "That'll be four dollars altogether."

"What? You're charging me fifty cents for six bullets?"

"Yep."

"Damn!" Ed groused. "A man sure gets scalped in a one-horse town."

"Quit complaining," Clint ordered patiently, "I read about your miners' union getting another fifty cents a day at the Northern Belle. What's that bring your daily wage up to?"

The miner scowled. "Six dollars," he muttered, "and we earn every red cent of it."

"Sure you do," Clint said, counting out the six fresh bullets for his stingy customer. "Just like I earn every cent of what I take into this shop."

Ed paid for the bullets. His eyes raised to a new leather holster that Clint had hanging on a peg over his workbench. "You still want ten dollars for that carved leather holster and cartridge belt?"

"Yep."

"That's highway robbery!"

"You say that every time you come into this shop," Clint said. "But you keep looking at that holster. Why don't you put yourself out of your misery and buy the damned thing before someone else does?"

"What would I do with a gunfighter's holster?"

"I don't know," Clint said, "but since you fancy it, you ought to buy it."

Ed shoved his newly oiled and cleaned six-gun behind his waistband. "I been carrying my hogleg behind my belt for twenty-some years. It's always been there when I need it in a hurry. If I was to take to wearing a fancy holster, why, someone might think I fancied myself a gunfighter or some fool thing. They might want to test my speed and I'd end up getting killed for certain."

"That's a fact," Clint said agreeably. "With those big old paws of yours, I imagine you have to wrestle pretty hard just to hold a knife and a fork."

Ed grinned for the first time as he stopped at the door to the gunsmith shop and turned. "That's pretty much the truth. But I tell you what, I think that holster is about the prettiest damn thing I ever saw. I'd be willing to go eight seventy-five."

"Nine dollars, and I'll fill the cartridge loops with fresh bullets," Clint countered.

"All right, then, dammit!" Ed groused. "Take every last dime a poor working man ever saved."

"Hell," Clint said with a laugh, "you've probably got a fat savings account at the bank."

"I wish. Let me have it."

Clint took down the new belt and holster. The cartridge belt held twenty-one rounds and Clint loaded every one before he handed it to the old miner. When Ed buckled

THE DEADLY DERRINGER   5

the belt around his waist and dropped his old six-gun into the stiff leather holster, Clint thought the man seemed to grow an inch taller with pride. Ed wiped his dusty boots on the backs of his pants legs and straightened his hat.

Stepping back, he asked, "Well, what do you think?"

"I think you need to wear the gun a little lower on your leg," he said. "Let the holster out a couple of notches."

"You mean like a gunfighter?"

"Like you know how to use it," Clint said, stepping around the counter to show Ed by example. "Look. See how low my gun hangs on my hip? It rests right about where the butt touches my wrist."

"Yeah, but you really are a gunfighter. On you, it looks like it was meant to be there. But on me . . . well, I probably look like a vain old fool."

"Nonsense," Clint said, taking it upon himself to adjust the weapon. "You just look like a man who should be respected."

"For a fact?"

"For a fact," Clint said.

The miner's callused fingertips caressed the fine leather carving. "I guess a man deserves a nice thing or two in his lifetime."

"No one would argue that," Clint said, opening his door and ushering the miner outside. "So why don't you just parade around town a little and show it off?"

"I guess I will for a fact!" Ed crowed. "By God, it's the finest holster and cartridge belt in Candelaria or . . . maybe all of Nevada!"

"No question about it," Clint said, stepping back into his shop before closing it for the evening. "Can I buy you a drink?"

"Aw," Ed said, "I think I'd better get something to eat first."

"Suit yourself," Clint said as he locked his door and headed off up town to the Red Dog Saloon where he enjoyed spending many of his free hours playing low-stakes poker and sipping Bull Dog beer made at Candelaria's own brewery.

The sun was still high and hot and as Clint trudged along, he met several other men in town who greeted him with respect.

"That bank loan is still yours if you want it," Mark Perryman, the town's most prominent banker, said in greeting. "You could buy that shop instead of rent it. Make yourself a real estate profit as well as earn a good living."

"No, thank you," Clint said. "I mean to leave this town before the real heat of summer."

Perryman, a heavyset man in his early forties, nodded his double chins. "Hell, I sure can't fault you for that. I'd leave too, if I didn't own the bank!" Perryman chuckled at his own humor and moved on past.

Clint continued up the street along the boardwalk, greeting those he approached. Up ahead of him half a block, he saw a young man and woman walking rapidly in his same direction. He could hear the man's voice and it was strident and angry. The woman was wearing a bonnet but Clint could see that she had blond hair.

Suddenly, the man jerked the young lady off her feet and dragged her in between some buildings. Clint heard the girl cry out and then he heard the unmistakable sound of flesh striking flesh.

The Gunsmith raced forward, his boots pounding down on the boardwalk. When he came to the place where the couple had disappeared, he saw the man slapping the girl up against the side of the building.

THE DEADLY DERRINGER 7

"Hey!" Clint shouted. "Stop that!"

The man turned, but not before he bounced the girl up against the wall. Clint could not see his face clearly because of the poor light. But the man was young, tall and broad-shouldered. He was dressed well, in a black suit, white shirt and black tie. Clint pegged the man as a high-stakes gambler.

"Stay out of this, mister, unless you want more trouble than you can handle."

Clint skidded to a halt. He looked past the man to the girl who was now bent over, cradling her face and weeping softly.

"Miss? Are you all right?"

"Mister, I said to butt out!" the man shouted. "Now I'm going to give you to the count of three and then I'm going to go for my gun. You want to be a dead hero, or what?"

Clint took a deep breath. "I can't abide a man who beats up on women," he said. "But before you start your count, I'm going to do you a bigger favor than you deserve. Walk out of here with your hands over your head and you can live."

The gambler was silent for a moment. "Just who in the hell do you think you are?"

"Clint Adams. They call me the Gunsmith. Now make up your mind whether you intend to live or die."

Clint could not see the gambler's expression change. But he did see the man's right hand jump away from the six-gun strapped on his narrow hip. "Now wait just a minute, Mr. Adams. I didn't know it was you or . . ."

"Shut up and walk!" Clint snapped. "I'm giving you to the count of three to get out of my sight."

The gambler swallowed loudly, his body shook with outrage. "This is my fiancée!"

"One," Clint said.

"We intend to be married. You can't..."

"Two..."

"All right!" the gambler shouted as he turned and started to hurry on through to a rear alley. "Joanna, I'll see you later!"

When the gambler was out of sight, Clint relaxed and then he moved over to the weeping girl. She smelled like roses but wept like a baby. "I'm sorry," he said. "Are you all right, miss?"

After several minutes, she managed to collect herself enough to nod.

"Here," Clint said, pulling out a clean handkerchief and giving it to the young lady, "let me escort you over to the doctor's office. He can take a look at you and..."

"No," she said, "I'll be fine."

"Can I at least walk you home?"

She nodded, sniffled, and then blew her nose in his handkerchief. Looking up at Clint, she said, "Who are you?"

Clint introduced himself.

"But I heard you tell Ian that you were also called the Gunsmith."

"That's right. I repair guns."

"You must do more than repair them," she said. "Judging from the way that Ian took off. I've never known him to back down from anyone."

"That surprises me," Clint said. "Most men who beat up on women are the worst kinds of coward."

"He's no coward, Mr. Adams. But neither is Ian Palmer a fool."

Clint frowned. "Why would you marry a man that knocks you around that way?"

THE DEADLY DERRINGER 9

"Because I love him with all my heart," she said, taking Clint's arm and walking with him back out to the boardwalk. "And he has some wonderful points. He's handsome and charming."

"Charming as a cornered weasel, I'd say."

Joanna stopped and turned to look up at Clint. "Ian and I are betrothed," she said. "He is a gambler with many intemperate habits and, worst of all, a violent temper."

"So I noticed."

"I will change that," she said.

"No, you won't. Good women always think they can change bad men, but they never do, anymore than a cat can change its stripes. Your fiancé slaps you around now. Later, he'll use his balled fists. You're too lovely a girl to fall into that kind of a trap."

Joanna *was* lovely. Her heart-shaped face, coupled with deep blue eyes and dimpled cheeks, made her look like a doll. She was wearing a blue dress with a white lace collar and the Gunsmith could tell by the way it fit that she was quite a well endowed young lady.

"I appreciate your concern," Joanna said, "but you don't know Ian. I think you are wrong. After we are wed, I'm sure that he will learn to control himself better. You see, he is very jealous. If I so much as even look at another man, he will fly into a rage."

"So where does that place me?"

"If I were you," she said, batting her long lashes, "I'd find a reason to leave Candelaria."

Clint smiled coldly. "Miss . . ."

"Rogers. Joanna Rogers."

"Well, Miss Rogers, I've never left a town in my life out of fear of another man. And I doubt very much if your fiancé is foolish enough to want to tangle with me.

He sure didn't a few minutes ago in that side alley."

Joanna Rogers nodded. "That's true. But you don't know Ian like I do. His pride won't allow this to pass without some kind of reprisal."

"Are you telling me to watch my back?"

"I'm telling you, for your own safety's sake, to leave Candelaria."

"I can't and won't."

"Then I'm very sorry and I take no responsibility for your safety."

Clint frowned. "Could I come calling on you sometime?"

"No."

"Why?"

"Because I love Ian and we are engaged."

Clint shook his head. "I don't understand how you could love a man like that. I really don't."

"Good day," she told him, managing a smile. "You are a real gentleman and I thank you for your misguided but very kind intervention."

Before Clint could say another word, Joanna Rogers was moving down the boardwalk.

Clint let her go a block until something made him go after her. Hell, he had to do something to save her from making such a tragic mistake as marrying a man like Ian Palmer.

Clint followed the young lady to the Davis Hotel, a small, modest two-story establishment on the east end of town. He watched Joanna disappear into the hotel and then he went inside.

"Sir?"

Clint turned to see a a prim but sharp-faced woman staring at him with her arms folded over her flat chest. "Yes, ma'am?"

"No gentlemen are allowed in this hotel. It is for ladies only."

"Oh." Clint smiled because he had expected that Joanna might be living with her fiancé. "That's good! Excellent rule!"

The guardian of Candelaria's few virtuous and therefore very precious women looked surprised. "Yes, I'm glad you agree. Now please leave."

"Can I call on your ladies?"

"Of course," the woman said in a snappish voice, "this isn't a convent, you know."

Clint laughed and then he turned and walked away with the rose scent of Joanna still strongly affecting his senses.

TWO

During the next week, Clint found every imaginable excuse to meet Joanna Rogers and learn more about her. He discovered that she was employed at Candelaria's only furniture store and so Clint suddenly became interested in buying a piece of furniture.

"What is it exactly that you need," Joanna finally said after showing the Gunsmith everything in the store at least twice.

"I was thinking about a desk. Yes," Clint said, spying a fine rolltop desk and moving over to inspect it closely.

"For your gunsmithing office?"

"Well, certainly," Clint said. "I have some records to keep."

Joanna's expression told him that she doubted his word.

He smiled disarmingly. "It's true! And I don't even have a desk right now. Why, all the papers, receipts and such are just laying scattered across my workbench. Oily invoices are not very professional looking."

"All right," Joanna said, glancing up toward the front of the store where her employer, Mr. Miller, stood frowning, "then you should seriously consider buying this fine desk. As you can see, the joints are tongue-and-grooved with the greatest degree of craftsmanship. They are held together by the finest glue and the wood is solid mahogany."

Clint raised and lowered the front several times. "It seems to be well made."

"Oh, it is. All our furniture comes from Boston."

"Is that a fact?" Clint could hardly tear his eyes from her face in order to look closely at the desk.

"That's right. It is shipped around Cape Horn and then delivered in San Francisco. From there, it is loaded on the Central Pacific Railroad and freighted to Reno. After that, it is loaded on wagons and brought all the way down here."

"Sounds like a lot of work."

"Yes, and, of course," Joanna said, "those freight charges have to be included in the price. But even so, it is a bargain at only two hundred dollars."

"Two hundred?" Clint swallowed and shifted nervously on his feet. "Actually, I was looking for something a little more inexpensive."

Joanna's smile faded. For a moment, she had allowed some excitement to grip her because a two-hundred-dollar sale would earn her a ten-dollar commission and the desk had been sitting here for nearly six months without so much as a glimmer of interest from a potential buyer.

"How inexpensive?"

Clint rubbed his jaw and made what he thought was a good show of carefully evaluating the question. "Oh, I guess I'd like a desk for something under fifty dollars."

"Fifty dollars?"

She appeared so disgusted that Clint hastily added, "Well, maybe I'd go as high as seventy-five. But Miss Rogers, I sure would like to take you to dinner tonight."

THE DEADLY DERRINGER

"I'm betrothed," she said, watching as her frowning employer began to edge nearer. "You aren't really interested in buying a thing, are you?"

"No," he confessed. "But if it takes a sale to get you to go out with me, then I'd be willing to spend a hundred." Clint smiled his most dazzling smile. "You ought to be flattered, Miss Rogers."

If she was flattered, it didn't show. Joanna sighed deeply. "You're wasting both your time and mine," she said abruptly. "And while I'm grateful and, yes, even flattered, I've already explained that I'm engaged to Ian and love him very much."

"He'd be your ruin!"

"That's *my* decision, Mr. Adams. I'm a grown woman of twenty-one and I don't need you to tell me who or what I . . ."

"Is there a problem here?" the owner of the furniture store asked in a crisp, businesslike manner.

"No, Mr. Miller," Joanna said, forcing a brilliant smile. "I was just telling Mr. Adams that all of our furniture is manufactured in Boston's best factories and then packaged and shipped directly to this store."

"Quite so, Mr. Adams." Miller frowned. "But I thought I'd heard that you intended to leave Candelaria soon—before the heat."

"Well, I may, but that doesn't mean that I don't need some furniture in the meantime."

"Perhaps," Miller said with an air of tolerance, "Miss Rogers can find other things to do and I can assist you in the choice of whatever it is you are considering."

Clint saw Joanna excuse herself and hurry away, looking none too happy with him. "Thanks," Clint said to the proprietor, "but I think I'd better be getting back to my shop. I just remembered I've got some work to do."

"So do we, Mr. Adams. So do we."

Clint flushed because Miller's words made it clear that he was not welcomed back.

The Gunsmith was just stepping out the door when he nearly bumped into Ian Palmer.

For a moment, the taller man stiffened in recognition and then he said, "Buying furniture for your little shop?"

"Maybe." Clint's eyes were cold.

"But I doubt it," Palmer said. "I've seen your . . . little rat's nest and you couldn't fit a barstool in there."

"At least I have a business," Clint said, plenty willing to plant his fist into the smirk on Ian Palmer's face. "All you have is a deck of cards, probably marked or shaved."

Palmer's cheeks burned and the flesh around his mouth went pale. "You may be a big man with a gun," the gambler said, "but you've no right to accuse me or anyone else of cheating. Not without proof."

"Perhaps, but you just smell fishy to me," Clint said, hoping to goad the man into a fight.

Palmer's Adam's apple worked up and down his throat and a twisted smile formed on his thin lips. "Sure, you'd like me to go for my gun."

He unbuttoned his suit coat and held it out from his sides. "As you can plainly see, Mr. Adams, I'm unarmed. Gun me down and you'd hang for murder."

"Then as soon as you've saved up a few dollars, you should come by my shop and buy a gun," Clint said as he passed by the man and walked down the street feeling the hair on the back of his neck tingle with a mixture of fear and anger. Fear that Ian Palmer might shoot him in the back with a hideout gun and anger because he knew the dandy was going inside to escort Joanna Rogers to lunch.

THE DEADLY DERRINGER 17

Late that evening, Clint was eating alone when he heard a single gunshot down the street. Clint shifted his chair around so that he could see out the front window of the Gold Dust Café. He saw men running down the street but he still had a piece of apple pie to finish for dessert and a last cup of coffee, so he didn't get to his feet. Besides, shootouts were commonplace in this town.

There was a sheriff, Douglas Prince was his name. He was a fat, slothful man who couldn't begin to keep law and order and if he'd tried very hard, he'd have been either gunned down or chased off. So about all Sheriff Prince did was to glad-hand folks around election time and lock up an occasional drunk when it involved no personal danger.

"Another killing, huh, Clint?" the owner of the café said.

Clint forked a mouthful of apple pie, chewed it thoughtfully and nodded. "Maybe it's just some drunk letting off some steam. At least, I hope that's the case."

But a few minutes later, that hope was swept away when a man came running into the café. "Mr. Adams! Mr. Adams. Ed Harding has been gunned down over at Chase's Saloon. He's dying and calling your name."

Clint jumped out of his seat and threw himself at the door. "What happened?" he yelled as he followed the man down the street at a run.

"I don't know! I heard that some gambler got to teasing Ed about that fancy new holster you sold him and Ed got so mad he challenged the man to a gunfight. Guess he didn't have a chance, though. A fancy new holster don't mean much of anything in a real gunfight."

Minutes later, Clint was slamming his way through a block of men to kneel beside Ed on the saloon floor. A large crowd had formed a circle around the dying miner.

Clint only had to take one quick glance at Ed's gray skin to know that there was no hope. Ed was struggling mightily to breathe and every breath he took was accompanied by the sound of wind sucking through the bullet hole in his lungs. The miner's eyes were already starting to glaze.

"Ed! It's me, Clint Adams. What happened?"

Ed's lips moved and a whisper caused frothy red bubbles to float across his mouth. Clint leaned closer to hear.

"He said that I was . . . was an old fool," Ed whispered. "That I didn't deserve to wear a nice holster."

"Who? Who said that?"

"Gambler named Palmer. He said you cheated me. That the holster was made out of cheap Mexican leather."

"He lied!" Clint said, trembling with anger. "But none of that should have mattered to you, Ed. You shouldn't have let him get under your skin."

"I shouldn't have . . . have bought anything so new and so pretty," Ed said, choking and beginning to really struggle for air.

"Take it easy," Clint said. "Just take it easy."

"I didn't even clear leather," Ed wheezed. "Goddamn holster got me . . . kilt!"

Clint watched as the miner's body stiffened. He heard Ed's worn bootheels do a rapid dance of death against the floor and then a long sigh escaped from Ed and he went limp.

The mayor of town was bending over. "I guess we all saw it," he said. "Ed shouldn't have let himself be riled like that so that he went for his gun first. Hell, Palmer waited for what seemed like a full second or two before he pulled his own gun. One bullet through the chest. That was all it took."

THE DEADLY DERRINGER 19

"Where is he?"

"Palmer?"

"Who the hell else would I be asking about!" Clint yelled, coming to his feet.

The mayor swallowed nervously. "He and several of his friends marched directly across the street to the sheriff's office. They said they wanted to swear out statements saying that Palmer fired only in self-defense. And he did."

Clint swung around and bulled his way through the crowd. He crossed the street and went into the sheriff's office. Palmer and two other fancy-suited gamblers were standing beside Sheriff Prince.

"Now hold on, Clint," the sheriff cautioned when he saw the look on the Gunsmith's face. "Don't you go off half-cocked!"

Clint marched across the office and when he came up to stand before Ian Palmer he said, "You and me, outside."

"Oh no," Palmer said. "I won't be goaded into getting myself gunned down. I'm not that big of a fool."

Clint drew back his hand and slapped Palmer so hard the bigger man's head snapped back and blood trickled down from the corner of his mouth."

"I said, outside."

Palmer shook his head. "I shot that old fool in self-defense. I got a saloon full of witnesses, Clint. You gun me down, you'll be tried for murder."

"I'll take my chances," Clint said. "You knew that that old man couldn't draw and shoot worth a damn. His hands were too thick from swinging a pick most of his life. And you knew that it was me that sold him that fancy cartridge belt and holster so you goaded him into a fight."

Palmer drew a monogrammed silk handkerchief from the inside of his coat pocket and wiped the blood from his lips and chin. "I knew nothing of the sort. The old fart was bragging about that holster and when I told him to shut up, he got belligerent. The next thing I knew, he was challenging me to stand up and draw my gun. I had no choice but to defend myself."

"Just as you've no damn choice right now," Clint said.

"Now wait just a damn minute!" the sheriff cried. "Mr. Palmer and his friends are prepared to sign. . . ."

"The hell with what they're prepared to sign!" Clint stormed. "It was murder."

The sheriff began to sweat profusely. "Be reasonable, Clint! You know that you can outdraw this man! Why, you'd be doing the same thing he did to old Ed! Two wrongs don't make a right. And you were a lawman too many years not to see the truth of what I'm saying."

Clint expelled a deep breath. The sheriff was right. Two wrongs didn't make a right. But a good old man who had probably had a little too much to drink was dead for no better reason than that he'd been proud of a beautiful leather holster.

Clint took a step back. "You and me," he said in a low, hard tone of voice. "There will come a day."

Palmer forced a stiff grin. "I guess there will. But *I'll* choose the time and the circumstances, not you. A smart gambler never bucks the odds."

"You already have," Clint said as he turned on his heel and stomped out of the sheriff's office.

THREE

"Clint," Joanna pleaded as they walked out toward the edge of town, "why won't you believe me when I say that I love Ian at the same time I'm scared to death that he's going to kill you?"

Clint shoved his hands into his pockets. "I believe you," he said slowly, "but that doesn't mean that I'm going to just give up and let that man destroy your life. And I don't understand why you can't see him for what he really is—a vain, violent bully."

They stopped on a low ridge. It was almost sundown and the lava ridges to the east of Candelaria glowed darkly. This, Clint decided, was as pretty as this country got.

Joanna found a rock and seated herself. "Let me tell you how Ian Palmer and I met. Perhaps then you will understand."

Clint bit back a caustic remark and found a rock of his own. He pulled his Stetson down low on his forehead and said, "I'm listening."

"The first time I saw Ian Palmer was at church."

"What?"

"It's true," she said. "Now let me finish."

Clint ground his teeth together. It was impossible to imagine that Palmer had ever set foot inside a church.

21

"Ian was praying because he'd been forced to kill a man over a card table. I remember seeing tears on his cheeks and the sun was streaming through a pane of stained glass high up above the altar. I remember how the light touched Ian's face and colored his tears like a rainbow. I never forgot that moment and I think I fell in love with him right then and there."

"But Joanna," Clint said with exasperation, "just because he had a moment of remorse, that doesn't mean that . . ."

She was not listening. "There was a revival meeting that day and the preacher gave a hellfire and brimstone sermon. I fell to my knees with everyone else. We were caught up in the wonder of the Lord. All of us. And then the preacher he called for the sinners to repent and be cleansed. I found myself beside the altar and beside Ian. We were both crying and confessing our sins. It was like. . . . like we were getting married right then and there—to God, and to each other."

Joanna heaved a deep sigh. "I never forgot that. I believed from that moment on that God had put Ian there to give me a purpose in life. I knew from the start he had intemperate habits, wild ways and a hard, yes, even a cruel streak. But it would not have happened that way without the Lord meaning for us to be together."

Clint shook his head with defeat. The moment he heard this account, he knew in his heart that he could not rock the misguided faith this beautiful young woman had in Ian Palmer. When someone believed they'd received a message directly from on high, there was nothing in this world that would convince them otherwise. Martyrs had always died for their beliefs.

Something, however, made Clint say, "What if the Lord was throwing his strongest temptation at you that very minute? What if, up on that altar, he was challenging you to resist Ian Palmer instead?"

"No!" Joanna lowered her voice. "No," she said again, carefully and to herself. "The Lord would not do that. He gave me Ian to reform."

Clint raised his hands, then dropped them to his sides in defeat. "I guess that's it, then," he said. "I can't change your mind. The only thing that will change your mind is Palmer himself. And he'll do that. He'll lie, and cheat, and beat you up and then he'll desert you in a year or so. He'll leave you destroyed and without faith or money."

Joanna came to her feet. "I'm sorry you worry about me so much. As I worry about you, Clint. But it will end come Friday."

Clint had been gazing off at the lava ridges. Now, he turned to look more closely at the young woman. "Why?"

"Because we're leaving Candelaria," she said. "We're going to Virginia City. Ian says he'll marry me there."

Joanna looked so happy that Clint didn't have the heart to say a word of objection. He'd tried his very damnedest to make this beautiful girl see the error of her thinking, but he'd failed.

"Well, aren't you going to say anything?" she asked, coming close and trying to make him smile.

"Congratulations," Clint managed to say. "I hope that you really can change him and that you'll both be very happy."

Joanna threw her arms around Clint's neck and hugged him tight. "Thank you," she whispered. "I know that you're worried and think that I'm an awful fool, but sometimes a woman can see the good in a man that is buried way down deep."

"Yeah," Clint said, pushing her back to arm's length and then taking her hand. "We'd best be returning to town before Ian realizes that we've gone out walking alone together."

"Yes," she said, suddenly looking worried. "If he saw us together out here, he'd go crazy. He's so jealous. I just want this to be our good-bye. I just wanted to explain to you why I feel so much in love with Ian and know that it was meant that we are to wed and live together always."

"Sure," Clint said, feeling miserable. "I appreciate the explanation. I guess it would have helped if I'd have heard it right from the start."

"There was never a chance before now. But . . . well," she said, taking his hand as they began to walk swiftly toward town, "I knew coming out here alone like this was something that I had to do before I said good-bye."

Clint didn't remember anything more of their conversation on the way back to town. What needed to be said had already been said and that was the end of it. It was very seldom that he was ever rejected by a woman and only once or twice in his life had he met a girl that attracted him so strongly as Joanna Rogers.

Why, if not for Ian Palmer, he might have eventually decided to marry her himself! And that was saying something that many a Western woman would not have believed.

They parted behind Garber's Livery after a quick hug and a whispered good-bye. Clint did not look back as he walked away and it was in his mind to go get drunk. It was not every day that a man had his heart broken or watched a girl as good and as beautiful throw her life away on a man not fit to tip his hat to her in greeting.

THE DEADLY DERRINGER 25

"The hell with it," Clint muttered as he headed up the back streets, a bitter taste in his mouth and a scowl on his lips.

"Hey, Gunsmith!"

Clint stopped in his tracks. He had been so agitated and lost in his own dark thoughts that he'd allowed his defenses to fail and now, the unmistakable voice of Ian Palmer and the cocking of his six-gun brought an ominous warning.

"Raise your hands high above your head," Ian said, "or I'll blow a hole in your back."

Clint did as he was told.

"Now, turn around slow."

Clint turned and saw the six-gun in Palmer's fist. He also saw the light of pure hatred shining in the man's eyes.

"So," Palmer said, "you been out for a walk with my fiancée."

Clint saw no point in denying the fact. "That's right."

"Did you finally do it to her?"

"Damn you!" Clint raged.

"You did, didn't you?" Palmer said, stepping forward. "You got her out there in the sagebrush alone and you fucked her in the dirt. Or maybe across some big, flat rock. Admit it!"

Clint's insides went ice cold. "Why don't you ask her yourself," he said, desperately seeking a way out of this no-win situation.

"I'm asking you," Palmer said. "I want to hear it from you before I gun you down right here in the alley."

"Hey!" a man yelled in a drunken voice as he staggered into the alley, blinked and then stopped to sway on his feet. He raised a bottle of whiskey to his lips, then took a long pull on the bottle before he squinted and said,

"That you, Palmer? And the Gunsmith? Why, what the hell is going on, fer gosh sakes?"

Palmer's eyes widened with shock and surprise. For a moment, he didn't know what to do. Then, he whirled and the six-gun belched lead. The drunk took two bullets, one in the gut and the second, mercifully, between his bloodshot eyes.

Clint's own hand was streaking down toward his gun but it had a long way to go from over his head. Palmer spun back around and his gun bucked in his fist. Clint felt the man's bullet strike him in the side and twist him around even as his own gun was coming up level. Clint unleashed a bullet and it was wide. He felt himself being hit again but his second shot was lucky and it knocked the gun spinning from Palmer's hand.

Clint collapsed to his knees. He felt weak and he struggled to raise his gun and put a final bullet through Ian Palmer's heart. The man was unarmed but the time for justice was at hand.

"I'm sending you a one-way ticket to hell!" Clint cried, raising his six-gun, which suddenly felt like it weighed a ton.

"The hell you say!" Palmer screamed as his arm shot out before him and, too late, Clint saw the deadly barrel of a two-shot derringer. It appeared as if by magic, so suddenly that Clint could hardly believe his eyes.

In a terrible moment of helpless desperation, Clint tried to raise his gun the last few inches but Palmer's derringer was dealing smoke and death. Clint felt himself being knocked over backward and falling.

And then, he was spinning into the vortex of a tornado, getting smaller and smaller as the sunlight became a pinpoint and vanished completely.

FOUR

Joanna allowed herself to be helped into the saddle. "I just don't understand why we have to leave in such a hurry," she said as Ian Palmer tied a large bedroll behind his cantle. "What's wrong?"

Ian glanced toward the livery door and tried to mask his anxiety. No one besides the drunk had seen him tailing the Gunsmith and the drunk was dead. For that matter, so was Adams. That being the case, he had nothing to fear. And yet, he was afraid. Clint Adams was a famous man and he had a lot of friends. For that reason alone, it was only prudent to make tracks out of Candelaria.

"Listen, Joanna," Ian said, trying to be patient. "There was a very sore loser at the card table. He called me a cheat and I had no choice but to gun him down."

The excitement and confusion in Joanna's expression was replaced with immediate alarm. "Did you draw first?"

"No."

"Then you acted in self-defense."

"That's not the way the dead man's friends will see it," Ian told her. "Honey, the best and safest thing for me to do is to leave Candelaria on the run. Now, you can either come with me or stay behind, but this town isn't healthy for me right now."

"I'll come," she said. "But I just wish I could have said good-bye to a few of my friends before taking my leave. They'll think it's awfully strange disappearing like this."

Ian's temper flashed. "So who the hell cares? You'll never see 'em again! Goddammit, we're going to be married and here you are bitching about having to leave without saying good-bye to some friends!"

"But . . ."

"Do you want friends, or a husband?"

Joanna looked away quickly, not wanting him to see the tears that sprang unbidden to her eyes. "I love you," she said, "and I want to marry you."

Most of the heat bled out of Ian's voice and he mounted his horse. "All right, then. Let's just get the hell out of Candelaria and we'll be married in Virginia City."

"You won't change your mind?"

"Hell, no."

"All right," she said, reining her horse in behind his and starting for the livery door.

But when Sheriff Douglas Prince stopped them just outside, Joanna grew alarmed. "It was self-defense, Sheriff. Ian had no choice but . . ."

"Shut up!" Ian snapped.

"I'd like a word with you in private," the sheriff said to Ian.

"Sure." Ian twisted around in his saddle. "Honey, ride back inside the livery and wait until I call you out."

"Will it be all right?"

"Everything will be just fine. Now, do as I tell you."

When she disappeared into the livery, the sheriff said, "You're leaving Candelaria kind of sudden-like, aren't you, Palmer?"

THE DEADLY DERRINGER

"No law against that, is there?"

"No. What was Miss Rogers talking about just now? Something about you acting in self-defense?"

"She was just talking about another time and place," Ian said, challenging the sheriff to call him a liar. "It has nothing to do with you or this town."

"I'll bet," Prince said. "I guess you heard that the Gunsmith was shot down."

"Oh, really?" Ian feigned a mocking surprise. "What a shame! And we were such good friends."

"Yeah, I know."

"Here," Ian said, digging a silver dollar out of his pants pocket and flipping it to the sheriff. "Use that to buy some flowers for his grave."

The sheriff pocketed the dollar. "He isn't dead yet, Ian. Doc Mead is working like a crazy man to keep him alive."

Ian's grin slipped badly. "How could he . . . I mean, how many times was he hit, for God's sake?"

"Four. But two of them were just grazes with plenty of blood but no real damage. The other two bullets are the ones that the doc's trying to remove. I guess they're the ones that are making it touch and go."

"And the doc really thinks Gunsmith has a chance?"

The sheriff shrugged his shoulders. "Who's to say? My thinking is that, if the doc hasn't given up, then there must be some chance that Adams will pull through."

Ian's hand passed before his eyes and then he looked down at the sheriff. "Well, I guess all a man can do is pray."

"For what?" Prince asked with a sly grin. "That the Gunsmith recovers?"

"I didn't say that, did I?"

"No," the sheriff grunted, "and I wouldn't believe it if you had."

"We'd best be on our way."

"Don't you think you ought to wait around and see if you're going to have to run looking over your shoulder the rest of your life?"

"No," Ian said, after a moment of consideration. "A man gets shot that bad, he's more than likely never to be the same again. Four bullets would suck the spirit out of anyone. So one way or the other, I don't think I got anything to worry about from Mr. Adams."

The sheriff stepped aside but not before saying, "Miss Rogers is a real fine girl. I hope you realize that she could have had her pick of any man in town."

"Yeah," Ian said hotly, "and I guess I know that you couldn't keep her out of your own dirty old mind, huh, Sheriff?"

Prince's round cheeks colored pink. "You don't deserve her," he said as Ian spurred his horse past. "You don't deserve her at all!"

When Ian rejoined Joanna, she said, "Is it about the man that accused you of cheating at cards?"

"Yeah," Ian said as he lined his horse out and put it to a trot in the direction of Virginia City.

Joanna forced her own horse after him. "Well, what happened?" she called as they passed out of town.

"The sheriff just wanted me to know that the man might live."

"Then . . ."

"Then nothing, dammit!" Ian swore. "Whether or not he lives or dies don't mean anything. We're finished with Candelaria. I'm taking you to the Comstock Lode where we can make some real money and have ourselves a high old time."

THE DEADLY DERRINGER 31

"And get married," she called.

"Yeah, and get marrried."

For three solid hours, Ian kept his horse to a hard trot that covered a lot of distance without winding his mount too badly. By that time, Joanna was so obviously suffering that she had to pull her own horse up to a walk.

"I can't keep up that pace," she said when Ian rode back to see what was wrong. "Can't we please walk?"

Ian noted the pinched lines about her mouth that said better than words how much pain she was in because of the hard pounding.

"Okay," he said, glancing up at the sun and judging it to be only a few hours until sundown. "We've got a long ride ahead of us the next couple of days. No use in wearing out these horses on the first day."

"Can we find water out here?"

"Sure. There's a stagecoach stop about eight miles up this road. We'll spend the night there and get an early start in the morning."

Joanna's spirits lifted. "It will sure feel good to climb down out of this saddle. I suppose the cooking has to be pretty decent."

"Not necessarily."

"Well, I could cook if we had food."

"You might have to anyway," Ian said. "I'm a little short of cash and we might have to do a few chores to earn feed and grain for these horses."

"That's fine," she added quickly. "I don't mind at all."

"Good."

"What will we do in Virginia City?"

"Same thing I always do, gamble. And if the luck of the cards is with me, then we'll live pretty fine. There are lots of things to do and see there, Joanna. I think you'll like it."

"I'm sure I will. And if we could just find a little cabin that I could fix up, then . . ."

"No. We'll live in a hotel."

"A hotel?"

"Sure. You got to remember that I do most of my work at night. That's when the real money flows across the tables."

"I see. But you always came to take me to lunch. Did you do that after staying up all night?"

"Yep, but as soon as you went back to work, I went back to my hotel room and slept until early evening. It'll be a little hard for you to adjust to my schedule at first, but you'll get used to it."

"I can't stay awake all night."

He scowled. "Then I guess we won't see a lot of each other."

Joanna was too upset to say much of anything more as they rode on until nearly sundown and came to the stage station.

A filthy stage station tender dressed in bib overalls stiff with grease greeted them without much enthusiasm. Through an open doorway of the station, which was a little stone house with a brush roof, Joanna could see an old Indian woman tending a cooking stove.

"You fixin' to spend the night?" the tender asked as he spat tobacco between a gap in his missing teeth.

"Yeah," Ian said, stepping down from his horse.

"Her, too?"

"That's right."

"Cost you two bits each to sleep in our beds."

"No thanks," Ian said. "We'll sleep out in the yard."

"Damned hard ground out there."

THE DEADLY DERRINGER 33

"We're tough."

"Sometimes there's rattlers slitherin' around out there, too. Just last week one bit a mule. Its leg swole up bigger than yours."

Joanna did not relish sleeping on the hard-packed dirt but she could endure it for a night if necessary. However, the thought of getting bitten by a rattlesnake gave her the shivers.

"Ian, maybe we should pay the man for his beds."

"No," Ian said flatly. "Not unless you want to be covered with lice in the morning."

The station tender spat more tobacco. "Them horses are lookin' all sucked up in the gut. You been ridin' 'em hard."

"That's right."

"Cost you two bits each for waterin' 'em and two bits for takin' a bath out back in the tub."

Ian's voice took on a hard edge. "Listen, mister, are you fixin' to get rich off of us? Because, if you are, you picked the wrong folks. We're low on money, same as you are."

The station tender hitched up his overalls. His boots were half torn apart and he wore no shirt, only the overalls. He was a tall, hawk-faced man with a three-day growth of beard with plenty of gray hair.

"If you're broke, you can just ride the hell on."

The man started to turn and go back inside the stone house but Ian's hand shot out and he grabbed the man by one of the straps that went over his bare shoulder. Ian nearly jerked the station tender off his feet.

"Listen you, we're tired and hungry! Now, you tell that old Indian woman to cook up some beans and whatever else you have. We'll pay you a dollar for feeding us and for baths and some extra grain and feed for the trail."

"Hell, no!" the station tender cried, tearing free.

"All right, a dollar and two bits and my woman does the cooking and cleaning. That's the best I'll do."

The man stared at Joanna for a long minute. "You cook good?"

"I can cook, yes."

"All right, then. Gimme the money," the man said, holding out a grimy hand.

"Half now, half in the morning when we leave after breakfast."

"Ain't nothin' been said about breakfast!"

Ian lost his temper. With a curse, he backhanded the station tender across the face, knocking the man up against his stone house. In an instant, the Indian woman was filling the doorway, a huge butcher knife in her fat brown hand. She screamed a curse in her own language and might have attacked Ian except that a derringer suddenly appeared in his fist.

Joanna saw the derringer appear as if from nowhere. Ian had just thrown his arm out as if he were raising a finger at the woman and there was the stubby-barreled little gun.

"Ian, no!"

He did not look back at her but kept his eyes on the squaw and the station tender who were both glaring at him with pure hatred.

"On second thought," Ian said, "we'll just take some food and cook our own meals. We'll have some grain for the horses, too."

The station tender wanted to tell him to go to hell but the little silver-plated derringer made him bite back his angry words. In the squaw's language, he barked orders and the Indian woman disappeared inside.

Five minutes later, she reappeared with a dirty grain sack and another filled with about two pounds of jerked

THE DEADLY DERRINGER 35

beef and a big loaf of sourdough bread.

"Here," the station tender said, "now give me the money."

Ian paid the man and then collected both sacks of food and grain. "I saw you got a pole corral around in back. That's where we'll be keeping ourselves and our horses tonight."

"I got two horses in there already."

"Get them out and tie them up for the night," Ian demanded. "Either that, or turn the damn things loose and let them roam around until we leave in the morning."

Spitting a hard, black stream of tobacco juice, the station tender stomped off around his stone house. He appeared several minutes later with two sorrel geldings, which he tied by his front door.

Ian, with a smirk on his lips, led his horse around to the back corral and Joanna followed him.

When they had watered and fed the horses, Ian reached into the sack and took a hunk of jerky. He pulled a knife from his pocket and cut the jerky into two equal hunks and carefully laid them on a rock. Next, he tore the loaf of sourdough bread in half and then he made two big sandwiches.

"Here," he said, extending one to Joanna. "Eat up."

She took the sandwich and tried to smile but failed. She'd been hoping for much better but she did not want to appear ungrateful.

Ian bit into the sandwich and chewed savagely and she watched as he swallowed, seeing a huge lump move down his throat. When Joanna tried to tear a piece of the jerky and bread free, she thought that she was biting down on a piece of old shoe leather.

He laughed at her discomfort. "Come on, honey, it isn't *that* tough."

"Yes, it is," she said, deciding to eat only the bread and make another attempt at the jerky when he wasn't watching.

Just before dark, Ian laid their bedrolls out beside the rickety old pole corral.

"But what about the rattlers?" Joanna asked nervously.

"That old sonofabitch was just trying to scare you. Rattlers stay away from people. They don't like us any better than we like them."

She was not entirely convinced. "Are you sure?"

"Yep."

Ian peeled off his sweaty shirt. Joanna had never seen him bare-chested and she looked away quickly.

He grabbed her hand. "What the hell is the matter with you? You've seen men before."

"Yes, my father and brothers."

"Well, I'm no different."

"Yes, you are," she said, eyes still averted.

"We're going to take a bath right now," he said, unbuttoning the front of her dress.

She tried to pull away from him. "Please, Ian! I don't want to do this. Not until after we're married. I told you I didn't!"

"We're just going to take a damn bath! Now stop fighting me and be sensible!"

Joanna felt her dress start to tear and, realizing that he would not be denied, she quit resisting. A moment later, she was down to her chemise.

"You going to take the rest of it off, or am I?"

"I'll bathe in what I have left on."

"The hell you will!" he growled, tearing her undergarments away and hurling them aside as she tried to hide herself.

"Damn," he whispered hoarsely, "you're even prettier undressed than I expected."

"Ian, please!"

With an animal sound in his throat, he tore off his own clothes except for his stockings. Then, he grabbed her and pulled her down on their bedroll.

Pushing her legs apart, he entered her violently. She screamed and he began to rut. "I love you and we're gonna be married, damn you! Shut up!"

Joanna stifled her cries and held him tight as he rutted on her like a crazed animal. She had often wondered what it would be like to make love to the man she loved and always, the idea had seemed wonderful. This was *not* wonderful. It was awful!

"Oh, please stop!" she cried.

"Just another minute, honey," he groaned as his lean hips pounded at her harder and faster. "Just . . . ahhhhh!"

She felt his warm seed fill her loins and his body began to jerk. He was so strong and his passion so great she thought that he was going to break her apart. For a moment, she could not breathe because of his crushing weight, but then it was over.

His breath was ragged and his chest was heaving as if he had run a long way. When he pushed up on his elbows and looked down at her, he said, "You didn't do much for your part of it, Joanna. I expect my wife to do more than lay still like a corpse."

"Damn you to hell!" she screamed up at him, trying to push him off of her.

He laughed in her face and slammed his hips into her until she whimpered and begged him to stop.

"Honey," he said, "when you told me you'd never had a man before, I didn't believe it. But I believe it now."

"Get off of me!"

"I'm gonna break you in like a filly I might want to ride. I'm going to teach you how to pleasure me like no woman ever has before. You're like a clean blackboard in a one-room schoolhouse. You got no marks on you yet and I'm going to fill up every inch of you, honey."

"Please," she whispered. "Leave me alone."

He chuckled and pushed himself off her. His manhood looked huge hanging over her and she could easily see why it had hurt so much when he used it to impale her.

"Come on," he said. "Let's take that bath we paid for."

He pulled her to her feet and when Joanna looked away, she saw the station tender and the Indian woman watching them.

With a cry of humiliation, Joanna picked up a rock and hurled it at the pair of grinning idiots. She missed, but her aim was good enough to send them shuffling back around the corner of the station and out of sight.

Joanna choked back her tears. She felt violated and degraded. Every romantic dream she'd ever dreamed was a sham. And worst of all, she was a soiled woman, now unfit for any decent man.

FIVE

Joanna did not speak much during the long, hard journey to the Comstock Lode. Two more nights on the trail were ordeals as Ian had his brutal way with her sore body. Afterward, Joanna cried herself to sleep, wondering what she had ever seen in such a gluttonous beast. For his part, Ian ignored her during the daytime.

Almost as painful to Joanna as Ian's lovemaking was the memory of the Gunsmith. When she thought of him, it was with great sadness in her heart because she now realized—too late—that he had been by far the better man. Again and again, Clint Adams had tried to warn her about Ian's true nature but his words had been ignored.

I deserve being raped and used like a barnyard animal, Joanna thought miserably. I had my choice of good men and I chose the worst. I had Clint Adams, who would have probably asked me to be his wife someday, but I turned my back on him and chose a scoundrel and I have no one to blame but myself.

"That's Dayton up ahead and the Comstock Lode is in those mountains just beyond," Ian said. "We'll be in Virginia City by nightfall."

Joanna nodded with relief. Maybe in Virginia City she could slip away and escape. Or at least find a brave lawman to help her get away from this animal.

"We're gonna make a lot of money up there," Ian said, more to himself than to Joanna. "I got a feeling that the luck is going to come my way."

Joanna said nothing. She was dirty, hot and ashamed. A big freight wagon passed them and she was too ashamed to even look up at the driver when he called a greeting.

"I'll buy you another dress if that's what's got you so upset," Ian said, reaching out and touching her cheek. "You're gonna help me make a lot of money up there, honey. And ain't no need to tell people that we're married. I sure ain't going to buy you no wedding ring."

"I wouldn't marry you now if you were the last living man on the face of the earth!" she said hotly.

Ian's handsome face contorted with a sneer. "You're mine now, Joanna. You're spoiled goods. No more pretty little virgin to swing her butt down the boardwalk. And I'll figure out how you can best make money for me. You can be sure of that much."

Joanna was suddenly filled with a new fear. What did this madman have in mind for her? Prostitution? Of course, what else?

"I'll never work for you!" she cried. "I hate you!"

In reply, Ian grabbed her by the arm and twisted it so hard that pain brought Joanna up in her stirrups.

"Let go of me!"

"Damn you! I ain't gonna marry no woman that screws like she was dead and cries half the night. What the hell is the matter, anyway?"

Joanna managed to tear her arm free. She lashed out with her long, heavy reins and struck Ian across the side of his face, raising a mean welt. Seeing the murderous look in his eye, she twisted her horse around and kicked it into a run after the ore wagon.

THE DEADLY DERRINGER 41

"Come back here, you bitch!" Ian screamed, spurring the faster of their two horses after her.

Joanna did overtake the ore wagon before Ian reached out and grabbed her reins. Tearing them out of her grasp and dallying them around his saddlehorn, he managed to stop their horses.

"Damn you!" he shouted, backhanding her so hard she was knocked from her horse and landed on the hard-packed road. Her breath exploded from her lungs and, for a terrifying moment, she lay thrashing, completely unable to breathe and sure that she was going to die.

Ian was off his horse and at her side in a moment. He turned her over and pounded hard on her back, between the shoulder blades. The pounding brought air to her tortured lungs and Joanna was almost sorry to realize that she would live.

"You fool!" Ian swore. "What the hell is the matter with you, pulling such a stupid stunt?"

"I hate you!" she choked. "I hate you more than I've ever hated anyone in my life!"

She expected he would strike her again or maybe even throttle her to death and it would have been a blessing. Instead, he laughed, picked her up and threw her back into the saddle.

"At least hatred will bring out some passion in you tonight," he said, a hand slipping up her dress to her thigh. "I'd rather have you fight me in bed than do nothing."

Joanna tried to slash at him again with the reins but he grabbed them from her and said, "I'll keep ahold of these until we find a livery where I can sell our horses for a stake."

"Say, mister!"

Both Ian and Joanna turned to see a heavyset and full-bearded freighter glaring down at them from the seat of the ore wagon. A Winchester rifle rested across his lap and it was no accident that the barrel was pointed in Ian's general direction.

"I seen you whop that pretty woman in the face just a minute ago! Maybe you better give her to me."

Ian planted his feet wide apart. "And maybe you just better drive that wagon on by before you get yourself in a whole lot more trouble than you want."

The freighter spat a stream of tobacco juice down at Ian's feet and some splattered his pants. "Seems to me, pretty woman, that you're traveling with a purely mean sonofabitch instead of a man. You want to come with Jed Thurl? I ain't no woman beater. I'd treat you real nice and if you didn't like me, I'd take you on to Salt Lake City. I'm an honorable man."

Joanna swallowed. Thurl was a brute, but she decided anything was better than being with Ian, who might very well kill her in a sudden fit of rage.

"I'll come with you," she heard herself say.

"The hell she will!"

The freighter's rifle snapped up and on line with Ian's chest. "Mister, you either let go of her reins or I'll pump a bullet through your gizzard."

"It isn't cocked," Ian said with a confident sneer as he swept back his coat to reveal the gun on his hip. "You're runnin' a bluff, knowing I can draw and kill you before you can cock that damned rifle."

"Try me," the freighter said with a toothy grin. "Just try me, you fancy-pantsed sonofabitch."

Joanna was sure that the freighter wasn't bluffing and her heart began to race. Ian must have come to the same conclusion because he moved his hands out from his sides.

"All right, you win, mister. The woman is all yours."

THE DEADLY DERRINGER 43

The freighter chuckled and said, "Come on, girl. I won't hurt you none. I got a mean look about me, but I'm a damn nice fella until someone like your friend there jerks my line."

Joanna swallowed. She looked sideways at Ian. "Just let me go," she whispered. "You don't need me to make money on the Comstock. You don't need me at all."

"You're making a real mistake," Ian told her in a surprisingly calm tone of voice. "That big bastard will be mean to you. He'll use you up on the road to Salt Lake City and then he'll probably sell you to the Paiutes for whatever he can get. You'll become a desert squaw."

"Shut up, damn you!" the freighter shouted.

Joanna felt sweat river down her spine even though it was not all that warm. She looked up at the freighter, suddenly unsure. "Mister, I just want to go back down to Candelaria where I have friends. So if you could take me out a few miles and let me hitch a ride back down south when we come across another wagon, that's what I'd want to do."

"Suits me fine," the freighter said. "Slavery died with the South. You'd be free to do whatever you wanted."

Joanna made her decision and dismounted. "Just put me out of your mind," she said, looking up at Ian. "Just forget about getting married and all that. I don't want to ever see you again."

"Ha!" the freighter barked. "You see that, she likes the looks of a real man better than a fancy dude like you. I'll take care of your woman, don't you worry none about that."

Joanna wasn't at all sure that she wasn't getting herself into an even worse situation by trusting the freighter but she'd made her decision and she was sure that there was no turning back. Ian Palmer was a vain man and she'd soiled his pride. He would make her pay dearly for that, if he didn't kill her outright.

"Just stretch up and give me your hand, little lady," the freighter said, reaching down.

The freighter made the mistake of shifting his rifle aside as he reached down and Joanna barely had time to shout a warning as Ian raised his arm and his hide out derringer slapped into the palm of his hand.

"Look out!" she cried.

The derringer banged twice and even as the freighter's fingers touched her own, Joanna saw two bloody explosions, one from the man's forehead, the other from his chest. She saw the freighter's eyes widen in amazement and his lips moved but there was no sound as he leaned farther and farther out and then pitched off his seat.

Joanna screamed and jumped aside as the body narrowly missed landing on her. When she looked down at the freighter, she saw that he was already dead. When she looked up at the cold anger in Ian's eyes, she wished that she were dead too.

"Step back away from your horse."

Joanna did not even consider disobeying him this time. Something told her that Ian was very close to killing her.

Ian dismounted and went to kneel by the freighter's side. He quickly searched the dead man's pockets and found a roll of money, a good pocketknife and a letter, which he did not bother to read but wadded up and threw away.

"Help me drag his body over there behind that brush."

Joanna did as she was told. The freighter was very heavy and it took quite an effort to drag him to cover.

Taking the dead man's pocketknife and selecting a blade, Ian cut a branch of sage and shoved it at Joanna. "Brush out all the tracks."

"What are you going to do?"

"I'm going to find out if there's anything valuable in this wagon, of course."

When Ian dropped back to the ground, he grabbed Joanna by the wrist and twisted it until she was forced whimpering to her knees. "From now on," he said, "I won't turn my back on you for a minute. Any thought I had of making things easy for you are gone. You're going to be my paying whore and, if I have to, I'll tie you to your bed and charge admission."

"No!" she cried.

"Get back on your horse," he said as he scooped up the freighter's Winchester, aimed it at her and pulled the trigger.

The rifle exploded and Joanna collapsed in a near faint as a slug passed her face by less than half an inch.

He fired twice more, once grassing the haunches of the lead team horse and sending the driverless freight wagon racing off down the dusty road.

Joanna could hear Ian's demented laughter and, for the first time, she realized that the handsome young gambler was not only evil, he was crazy.

SIX

Joanna's spirits lifted as they rode slowly up the winding and heavily congested dirt road leading up Gold Canyon toward Virginia City. Behind them lay the Carson River now clogged with timber cut and floated off the Sierras. Huge sawmills with their steam-driven engines cut millions of board feet of mine timbering for the Comstock Lode.

It was made very obvious to Joanna that Ian had been here before and knew quite a bit about deep-rock mining. "The forty-niner gold rush, now that was kid's stuff compared to what we have here. In California, it was all placer mining where a man needed nothing more than a pan or a rickety old sluice box to get rich. But here, on the Comstock Lode, the gold and silver ran in veins then, fifteen feet wide. Some of them are more than a thousand feet below the surface."

Ian pointed down at the road. "Why, I wouldn't be surprised if there were some poor sonsabitches beating rocks right underneath us."

Joanna glanced down, then back up again quickly. She did not care about the Comstock Lode. Her most immediate concern was her life.

"What do you think you're going to do with me up here?"

"I'll hang onto you until you make me a big sack of money, then I'll turn you loose."

"I won't be your... your whore," she stammered. "You can strangle me, shoot me or cut my throat, but I won't do that."

"We can talk about it later," he growled. "Right now, we're coming up to Devil's Gate. Now, don't try to do anything stupid when the toll man comes out to collect money. I don't expect you want any more men dying on account of you."

"No," Joanna whispered, thinking of the poor freighter. She would never know for sure whether or not his intentions had been honorable but, unquestionably, he'd died attempting to help her.

Devil's Gate was a narrow, fifty- or sixty-foot wedge in the canyon through which all traffic had to pass.

"It's owned by some lucky sonofabitch," Ian groused, "and he charges two bits a horseman and a dollar a wagon. You can just bet he's getting rich."

Joanna could see that two riflemen were posted up above. "They don't take no for an answer," she said.

"That's right. No one knows if they'd actually shoot down someone who tried to charge through this gap without paying, but I suspect they would. If they showed one man mercy then everyone would call their bluff and the gate would be worthless."

"Afternoon," a man said as he came out of a little wooden shack by the entrance. "Be a dollar for you and another for the lady."

Ian stiffened. "That's a hell of a steep jump from the last time I rode through here!"

THE DEADLY DERRINGER 49

The toll taker just shrugged his shoulders. "I don't set the rates, mister. I just collect the tolls. Now, you and the lady don't want to pay, you can sure as hell ride back down to the Carson Valley, then come up Six Mile Canyon from the north. There's no toll that way."

"It's also a day's ride out of our way."

"Well, then," the man said, "you have to ask yourself if it's worth saving a dollar for a day's hard riding for you and the pretty lady. I'm betting it isn't."

Ian was furious, but he paid the two dollars and they rode on through, but not until the toll keeper had waved up to his riflemen.

"It's robbery is what it is," Ian swore as they passed through and continued up the canyon.

About a mile farther, they came into a crowded little mining town. "This is Gold Hill," Ian said. "And from what I can remember, it's about doubled in size since the last time I was here."

To their right was a brewery and several saloons with dozens of rough and dirty-looking miners who stared at Joanna with hot eyes. She kept her own eyes straight ahead, even when men whistled at her in admiration.

"See there," Ian whispered, leaning close. "Even in a torn and dirty dress, with your hair all tangled and full of stickers, you're still plenty pretty enough to attract all this attention."

"I hate it!"

"Sure you do," he said in a mocking voice. "Just the same as I hate it when women give me a bold eye."

"I *do* hate it!" she cried.

"Better get used to it," he said. "Up on the Comstock, there are only two kinds of women—respectable and the other kind. And since you told me you wouldn't marry me even if I were the last man on the face of the earth, you're going to be one of the 'other kind,' and they attract all the whistles and attention."

Joanna felt hot tears burn her eyes. "When will you let me go?" she asked as they rode past the Gold Hill Hotel and she saw two ugly and half-dressed blond floozies leaning over the upstairs balcony and studying her with ill-concealed jealousy.

"When you make me . . . oh, five thousand dollars, then I'll let you go," he said as if he were doing her some huge favor.

"Five thousand dollars! Why, that's more money than I'll ever see in my life!"

"Not up here it won't be," he said. "If we handle you right, you might be able to make that the first year. I'm going to buy you some nice clothes and see that you meet rich men. You're too damn pretty to be layin' down for a dollar a poke."

"I told you that I'm not doing that—not for rich, or poor men."

"Oh," he said, " you'll do it all right. And if you ever get it in your mind how to please a man, then you'll make that five thousand dollars in no time at all with your looks. Why, hell, Joanna, if you put your heart into your work, you could end up owning your own whorehouse! You could become a rich madam with a dozen or so girls all working for you."

Ian laughed outright at this image but Joanna shuddered. He was so confident, cunning and ruthless, she felt her spirits plummet because she might never escape his clutches. They passed by the Gold Hill Daily News office and the road grew very steep.

"What we got ahead of us is a real steep climb," Ian said, "and then we cross over the top of the Divide and drop down into Virginia City. That's when you're really

THE DEADLY DERRINGER 51

going to see something that will pop your eyes out."

The last few hundred yards up and over the Divide were terribly steep and Joanna could feel her poor mount's heart thumping like a drum before they crested the peak and reined over to the side of the road to take in the sight.

Ian had not been exaggerating about Virginia City. It was magnificent! Everywhere she looked, Joanna saw men hard at work building and digging in the mountainside. A tall, white steeple glistened in the high desert air.

"A church," she whispered. "What denomination is it?"

"Roman Catholic. It's called St. Mary's of the Mountains."

"It's beautiful."

"Over there is the Ophir Mine and to its left where that huge building rests is the Chollar Mine."

As Joanna sat her puffing horse, Ian ticked off the names of the other huge mines with their stacks belching smoke so that their monstrous steam engines could turn the mighty flywheels needed to raise and lower miners up and down the deep shafts.

"Gould and Curry, there, Comstock Mine over there, Hale and Norcross about a mile to the west. Those are the biggest and they keep miners working twenty-four hours a day. That means lots of wages and easy pickings for a man with the talent and guts to use a deck of marked cards."

"Then you cheat." It shouldn't have surprised her, but somehow, it did.

"You have to cheat," Ian said. "Every professional needs his edge. If I'm playing against easy marks, I play honest. But whenever another professional deals into the game, it's just understood that the cleverest and best cheater is going to win the pot."

"And what happens if you're caught?"

Ian shrugged. "If someone calls you for cheating, they have to expect to pull their gun. That's why I have this special derringer rigged up my sleeve. It's my own design and I've never seen one to deliver a gun any surer or quicker."

"It's your edge," she said.

"That's right. If a man thinks he can prove I'm cheating and I suspect he really can, then I'll challenge him to draw his gun. He might decide to do it, or he might not. It's a matter of guts and I've got more than my share."

Joanna looked away. He called it guts, she called it being ruthless and without conscience.

"We'll check into the Delta House," he said. "It's clean and they'll bring us a hot bath. After that, we'll use the money I make from the sale of these horses and saddles to get us some new clothes and something to eat. You look pretty starved, Joanna."

She was hungry. In fact, she was absolutely famished. Ian reached out and touched her cheek. "I shouldn't have backhanded you so hard," he admitted. "Your cheek is bruised and we'll need to get some powder to hide that."

"Let it show," she said in her coldest tone of voice. "I want people to know what kind of a bully you really are."

"Ha!" he laughed, reaching out and grabbing her by the hair and almost dragging her out of her saddle to bruise her lips in a hard, grinding kiss.

"Let go of me!"

He shoved her away. "Honey, you've got a hell of a lot to learn and earn before I turn you loose, so the sooner you get started, the better it will be for everyone."

"I'll get away from you somehow!"

"If you try on your own, I'll hunt you down and kill you. If you get help from some poor devil, I'll kill him just like I killed that freighter a few hours ago. Think about it real carefully, Miss Rogers."

Joanna turned her head away and he took her reins and led her horse off toward Virginia City. In all her life, she had never felt so hopeless or defeated.

SEVEN

Dr. William Mead leaned closer and lifted the Gunsmith's eyelids to examine his pupils. One of the four bullets fired had dug a furrow across the side of the Clint's skull, a rather deep furrow that actually penetrated the cranial cavity and might have caused substantial brain damage. The other life-threatening wound was in the Gunsmith's side where the doctor was concerned it might have punctured his patient's kidney and caused internal bleeding. That, however, had not been the case or Clint would have died weeks ago.

The doctor glanced sideways at his nurse, a young spinster in her early thirties. Miss Alice Duncan was nearsighted and so her appearance was hampered by thick glasses. Her long, brown hair was braided and tied in a bun at the nape of what the doctor suspected was a lovely neck leading down to an even lovelier body.

"I don't have any notion at all whether or not this patient will completely recover his mental faculties," Dr. Mead said.

Alice Duncan said, "You mean that he might never regain consciousness?"

"That is always a possibility with this kind of head injury," Dr. Mead sighed. "And if that is the case, it would be far better if he were dead than permanently brain damaged."

Clint had been hearing voices for the past hour and now his head rolled back and forth and he opened his eyes. "I'm not brain damaged," he whispered.

Both the doctor and the nurse displayed astonishment. Dr. Mead cried, "How long have you been conscious?"

"I just woke up," Clint said. "What happened?"

"Don't you remember?"

The Gunsmith frowned. "No," he said after a long pause. "I remember falling and that's the last thing I remember. But there was a young lady. Her name is . . . is Joanna Rogers."

"Don't struggle," the doctor said with concern. "Some things will come back to you on their own."

Clint tried to sit up and look around. "Where is she?"

"She left town weeks ago. Probably with that gambler, Ian Palmer. It was all rather sudden, wasn't it, Nurse Duncan?"

"Yes," she said, pushing Clint back down flat on the bed. "But I really didn't take much notice of it. And Mr. Adams, you're going to have to lie still or you might have violent headaches. Isn't that right, Doctor?"

"Most certainly." The doctor fingered the stethoscope which dangled at his chest. "Mr. Adams, you have been shot four times. The most serious wounds were in the head and the side. Frankly, you are lucky to be alive. And except for an apparent loss of some memory, you appear to be in excellent condition. It's all quite remarkable, really, considering what you've been through."

"Who shot me?" Clint asked, fingering the bandage wrapped about his head.

"I don't think anyone knows. The town drunk, poor Willard Myers, was also gunned down. Does that help you with any mental connection?"

"No," Clint said after a long pause. "I don't remember anything except that I was walking back into town and then . . . then it's all a blank."

"Sheriff Prince asked some questions around town. But he couldn't find anyone who could give any clues about who shot you or poor Willard."

Clint scowled. "I don't remember the sheriff."

"Maybe you will once you see him. The mind often works like that, you know."

"Then perhaps I'd also recognize the man that shot me," Clint said.

"It's possible." Dr. Mead could only shrug his shoulders. "We know practically nothing about the mysteries of the brain. There is such a thing as selective amnesia."

"What's that?"

"Sometimes the mind simply blanks out in moments of great stress and, as in your case where you were gunned down and probably conscious when being fired on again and again, it is not inconceivable that your mind shut down in self-defense."

Clint brushed his hands across his eyes. "Is there any way to reach back?"

"There might be," the doctor said. "Very little is known or understood. I've only seen a few instances of amnesia. In one case, full memory was restored after only a few months. In another, the patient never really did remember being attacked and raped. And I think that it was a blessing. There are some things best forgotten."

"This isn't one of them," Clint said. "Someone gunned me down and left in a hurry, probably sure that I was dead or dying. If that someone is still around, I need to recognize them before they try to finish me off."

"I understand," the doctor said, "and I sympathize. But you have been unconscious for over two weeks and you are weak. You've been through a great ordeal. The main thing now is to regain your strength."

Clint expelled a deep breath. "I have a gunsmith shop, don't I?"

"Yes."

"And a bank account?"

"Nurse Duncan and I certainly hope so."

"I do have one," Clint said. "And you will be paid in full."

"It might lift your spirits to know that the townspeople have taken up a collection for you and Willard. Of course, Willard's part of it went toward a headstone. But your part totaled almost one hundred fifty dollars and that will cover your medical payments and recovery for another week or two."

"Good," Clint said, his mind churning as he tried to remember what he and Miss Joanna Rogers had talked about just a short while before his blackout.

"Miss Duncan will try to make you as comfortable as she can. She is very good with recovering patients."

For the first time, Clint really looked at the woman. He decided she would actually be quite attractive if she removed her glasses and let her hair down.

"Miss Duncan," he said, "I'll try to be an agreeable patient."

"I'm sure you will be."

Clint turned back to the doctor. "I'd like to get up and start asking some questions around town just as soon as possible."

"If you push yourself too hard, you could have a severe setback."

THE DEADLY DERRINGER 59

"That's a chance I'm willing to take," Clint said. "And if I've got to spend time in bed, I'd rather it be my own bed."

"I'd rather you remained here at my house and adjoining office where Miss Duncan can watch you more closely," Mead said. "At least for a couple of days."

Clint didn't like the idea but he nodded. "All right. But if I'm up and about in two days, then I'm moving back to my hotel room."

"Very well," the doctor said, dismissing the matter. "I've got patients to visit. Miss Duncan will be nearby if you need her."

When the doctor walked away, Clint looked at Miss Duncan. "You going to tell me bedtime stories, or what?"

She smiled and it made her almost pretty. "I don't know any bedtime stories. But I will read to you."

But Clint shook his head. "Later, maybe. Right now, though, I need to try and do some remembering."

"Maybe you shouldn't," Nurse Duncan said. "It might be too much for you."

Clint shook his head. "Someone gunned me down and I'd better remember before I see them again. At this very moment they might be coming to finish the job. Your own life could be in some degree of danger, Miss Duncan."

Her eyes widened. "I . . . I hope not," she whispered. "But if that is the case, then I'll just have to trust that my time hasn't come yet."

As soon as Clint was able to get back on his feet, he paid a visit to Sheriff Prince. When the Gunsmith walked into the sheriff's office, the man was dozing in his chair, feet up on his desk. Clint shook his head with disgust. In all the years that he had been a lawman, he'd tried to be as professional as possible. A sheriff, even one like Douglas

Prince, who probably didn't get any respect and damn little money, still owed it to the law profession to act like a man who deserved a badge and the trust of the people.

Clint swatted Prince's boots, practically knocking them from the desk. The pudgy sheriff started badly and almost spilled over backward in his creaky office chair.

"What the hell?" he blustered, slamming his boots to the floor and trying to pull himself together. "You shouldn't startle a sleeping man thataway!"

"And you shouldn't be sleeping while at work," Clint said, taking the only other chair in the office.

Prince muttered something that Clint chose to ignore. "I come to find out if you know who shot me and that other fella down."

Prince knuckled the sleep from his eyes. "I'm still conducting the investigation," he said. "There were no witnesses so I haven't had anything to go on."

"And you aren't doing much to dig up anything, are you?" Clint demanded.

"Now, just a damn minute!"

Clint came out of his chair. "Listen up," he grated, hovering over the sheriff. "You're worthless as tits on a boar hog, everyone knows that. But I got a hunch you have got at least some idea who shot me down, so let's hear it!"

Sheriff Prince stared up into Clint's eyes and his mouth went dry with fear. "Why don't you just simmer down a little and settle back in that chair so we can talk in a calm manner instead of shouting."

Clint sat down. "Who was it?"

Prince sighed. "The thing of it is, Gunsmith, I got no proof."

Clint's anger flared again. "I'm not asking for proof! I'm asking you to tell me what you know. Everyone I've

THE DEADLY DERRINGER

talked to so far says that it was probably that two-bit gambler, Ian Palmer. Is that what you think?"

Prince nodded his head.

"But how did he get the drop on me and where did he go?"

"He's probably damn fast and has a hideout gun on him," Prince said. "Either that, or you were suddenly distracted and he was lucky enough to get off the first bullet that dropped you."

Clint stood up and paced the floor. "I can't remember anything. I don't even remember what the man looked like."

"Do you remember what Miss Rogers looked like?"

Clint shook his head.

The sheriff clucked his tongue with regret. "Your brain really did take a lickin', then, because Joanna Rogers was the kind of looker that even an old man wouldn't soon forget."

"Describe her."

"Medium height. Blond hair, prettier than gold, bright blue eyes and perfect teeth. A smile that makes a man weak in the knees. She was a fine young lady." The sheriff sighed. "She was the kind of girl that I wished I would have met when I was in my early twenties. I'd have courted her and asked her to marry me."

"But instead, she chose Ian Palmer. Why?"

"He's a big, rugged, handsome bastard," the sheriff said a little enviously. "Damn whores over on Stoner Street would lay down with him for free. He was a lady's man for sure. Dressed in a nice suit, fancy white silk shirt. He could charm the hide off a horse and he promised to marry Miss Rogers."

"Did you see them leave town together?"

"Yeah."

"And you didn't even try to interrogate him about the shooting?" Clint demanded, his voice taking on a hard, challenging edge. "Why not?"

Prince reached into his desk drawer. He pulled out a pint of whiskey and offered some to Clint. When his offer was declined, he said, "Mister, you're the Gunsmith and Ian Palmer managed to damn near kill you. Now just what the hell kind of a fighting chance do you think a man like me would have?"

"Not much," Clint said, the heat draining out of him. Prince was right, he was no match for the gambler and would only have gotten himself shot. "So where were they heading?"

"The Comstock Lode," the sheriff said. "I overheard that much while they were saddling their horses in the livery barn. The bastard promised Miss Rogers that he'd marry her in Virginia City."

"But he won't," Clint said. "A real lady's man like that couldn't take being tied down to the responsibilities of marriage. He'd know that right down in his gut."

"He'll break her heart and her spirit," the sheriff said sadly. "Be a hell of a tragedy."

"You should have gunned him down even it if was from ambush," Clint said as he turned to leave. "But instead, you let him ride away free."

"This town only pays me twenty-five lousy dollars a month," Prince said bitterly. "Twenty-five and found."

Clint's mouth curled with derision. "You're overpaid at that, Sheriff," he growled as he turned and stomped toward the door.

"You going after him?"

Clint flung the door open. "You're damn right I am."

EIGHT

The Gunsmith had planned on leaving Candelaria the same afternoon he'd confronted the sheriff, but he'd overestimated his physical ability and underestimated the extent of his injury. So much so that, by the time he returned to his room at the doctor's office, he was experiencing blinding headaches that left him grinding his teeth in pain.

"You must come to bed immediately!" Nurse Alice Duncan exclaimed after taking one glance at his pale, sweating face.

Clint did not have the strength to argue. He allowed the nurse to remove his shirt. "Help me get my boots off and I'll do the rest."

A few minutes later, he was being tucked into bed and given some medicine. Nurse Duncan was a soothing angel. "The doctor is out on a house call but he should return in a few hours—if everything goes well."

"What's that supposed to mean?"

"It means that Mrs. Winnie Evans, who is only seventeen, is having her first baby and she might have some difficulty. You see, she stands only about five feet tall, while her husband is well over six feet."

"I understand," Clint said, starting to feel a little better. "And I want you to know that I appreciate your help. I don't know what came over me."

"I do. You've suffered very serious cranial damage. Mr. Adams, you can't just expect to pick up where you left off. It's like Dr. Mead said, it will take weeks, possibly months, before you recover."

"I can't afford to spend that much time recovering," he told her. "You see, I know who shot me."

Nurse Duncan raised her eyebrows. "Oh, really? Who?"

"Ian Palmer, the gambler. The sheriff as much as admitted that he was the one."

"Then why was the man allowed to leave Candelaria?"

"Sheriff Douglas Prince leaves a whole lot to be desired as a lawman—or even a man, for that matter. Anyway, he said that he overheard the gambler promise to marry Miss Rogers in Virginia City. I need to get there before that happens."

"Impossible. Besides," the nurse said, "if the girl chooses to run off with a murderer, then she has probably already decided to marry him."

"But he *won't* marry her," Clint argued. "He'll just destroy her and then throw her away without decency or pride."

The nurse removed her glasses and stared at Clint. "My dear Mr. Adams, I think you underestimate the strength and resilience of women. Now, I did not know your Miss Rogers very well, I admit that. But I did see her occasionally and she struck me as a young woman very capable of making her own decisions and taking care of her own needs."

"She had a real innocence," Clint said. "Most women in these mining camps are hard. They've been used and

THE DEADLY DERRINGER 65

often mistreated. But Miss Rogers, well, she was kind of fresh and wholesome." Clint smiled boyishly. "Like you, Miss Duncan."

"I'm thirty-three years old. That's hardly fresh anymore."

"With those thick glasses off, you look as if you were in your twenties."

She smiled radiantly. "Well, thank you!"

"And I'll bet," Clint said, pressing forward as his headache disappeared, "that you would look even younger if your hair wasn't so severely tied behind your head."

She blushed. "I don't know about that. Dr. Mead would be very upset if my hair ever got in the way of treating a patient. It's really quite long."

"I'd like to see it down sometime," Clint said, taking the nurse's hand. "What do you say about that?"

Nurse Duncan swallowed dryly but she did not pull her hand away. "I . . . I really do have nice hair," she managed to say. "When I was a girl, I always thought it was my best feature."

"I'm sure it's quite beautiful," Clint said, releasing her hand and touching her cheek. "Have you ever been married before, Miss Duncan?"

"Once." She reached up and unpinned her hair. "But my husband was killed by Indians just a few months after we were married. He was a fine man."

Her hair tumbled down and she tossed it with a shake of her head. Clint reached up and stroked her dark, lustrous mane with his fingers. "It's the color of polished mahogany wood."

She leaned forward, lips wet and parted. "Do you really think it's beautiful?"

"Very," Clint said, feeling his manhood rise as his hand touched the mound of her breasts and she closed her eyes and bit her lower lip. "It is very, very beautiful."

"He never noticed," she whispered.

"Who? Your late husband?"

"No, Dr. Mead."

"Oh," Clint said as he began to unbutton her blouse. "Well, then, maybe you ought to just let it down and show him sometime."

She opened her eyes. "Do you really think so?"

"I do."

"Hurry," she whispered, wiggling her body and reaching under the sheets to stoke Clint's bare leg. "I don't know when he'll be back."

"First deliveries are never that fast," Clint said, as he finally got the buttons undone.

A moment later, Nurse Duncan was throwing her dress aside and tearing off her underclothes. "This is insane!" she cried, slipping under the sheet and into Clint's waiting arms.

"It's just what the doctor should have ordered," he said, nuzzling her neck and trailing his lips down across her lush breasts.

She was panting. "I haven't had a man since my husband, thirteen years ago."

"What a waste," he murmured as he lightly tongued her hardening nipples.

"Yeah," she moaned as she climbed onto him and guided Clint's swollen root into herself, "isn't it, though?"

Clint groaned with pleasure as the nurse's hips began to rotate. "Are you in love with Dr. Mead?"

"I have been for ten years."

"Maybe you ought to seduce him before any more time passes," Clint said, reaching down to grip her buttocks and pull her against him with even greater force.

THE DEADLY DERRINGER 67

"Yeah," she said, "what do I have to lose by trying, huh?"

"Exactly," Clint said, gritting his teeth with pleasure and growling low in his throat.

Nurse Duncan also began to make soft, animal sounds as her sleek hips rotated faster and faster. The Gunsmith rolled her over and in the last frantic minutes of their union, he brought Alice to the point of shivering ecstasy. She cried out with pleasure, milking him to a shuddering collapse.

For several minutes, they both lay spent, slick with sweat and heaving for breath. She looked up at him, eyes still glazed with passion. "I sure wish you would remain my patient for at least another few weeks."

"I just can't," he said honestly. "You know that I'd like to. You're a wonderful lover and very beautiful, too. But Miss Rogers will be destroyed if I don't help her."

Alice nodded. "I understand. Will you come back after you rescue her?"

"I might."

"But you'll be in love with her."

"I don't know. Why don't we see what happens. You might be married to Dr. Mead by then."

"He doesn't even think of me as a woman."

Clint bumped his hips against hers. "If you seduce him he most definitely will."

"What do I have to lose?" she whispered, kissing him passionately and then breaking away to whisper, "After this, I can't live without love anymore. I'll have to find a man."

"Maybe that's for the better," Clint said tenderly. "Alice, you're just too handsome a woman to go to waste."

A tear glistened in her eye. "First babies take forever," she said, "do you think we have time to do it all over again?"

Clint laughed. "Yet bet we do, Nurse. Maybe even a couple of times."

"Mmmm," she sighed. "Why didn't you get shot ten years ago?"

Clint didn't have a ready answer for that so he raised up a little and his mouth found her breasts again. In very short order, Alice's nipples were hard and peaked and she was starting to breathe rapidly.

"You know what I think?" she panted.

"What?"

"I think that this could be habit-forming."

"I *know* that it can be," he said with a chuckle deep in his throat.

Clint wasted no more time as he took Alice again. He took her slowly and built her up until she was half out of her mind with desire, then he satisfied her before he satisfied himself.

Later, she breathed, "When will you have to leave Candelaria?"

"In a couple of days," he decided out loud. "Coming back from the sheriff's office, I almost passed out when I was struck by that headache."

"But it's gone now."

"You made my brain think only pleasure."

Nurse Duncan's eyes sparkled with mirth and she said, "Now, that is probably not the kind of treatment that the medical profession would prescribe."

"Only because they are all men."

"Yes," she said, nuzzling his neck. "And even that will someday change."

Clint believed her. But that was the future and this

THE DEADLY DERRINGER 69

was good and it was now. Dr. Mead had only been gone about an hour. As far as he was concerned, they still had plenty of time for several more repeat performances, if he was up for it.

Three days later as Clint was stuffing his saddlebags in preparation of leaving, Alice Duncan came rushing into his room. Throwing her arms around his neck, she cried, "You've given me so much!"

Clint held her for a moment and then he pushed her back to arm's length. During the past three days, he had lost track of the number of times he'd made love to Alice but he could see that she had changed. Her hair was down, her utilitarian glasses had been replaced by new, attractive frames which complemented rather than detracted from her now-radiant appearance.

"You are not the same woman you were when we met."

"I feel beautiful now, thanks to you."

"It shows."

"It must," she said, blushing with joy, "because this morning, Dr. Mead asked me if he could take me out to dinner and then to a dance over at the town hall. Do you know what that means?"

Clint shook his head.

"It means he is making a public statement that I am his . . . his girl and that everyone in town should realize it."

"Seduce him tonight and he will propose marriage to you by tomorrow."

"Do you really think so?"

"I'm sure of it."

"Then I'll do it!" she cried, kissing him again.

Clint grinned with delight. He would bet almost anything that, after ten years, Alice was finally going to get her man. And if the doctor wasn't smart enough to propose marriage, someone else would very, very soon.

Alice Duncan, quite obviously, was a new woman who was going to be attracting a lot of male attention in the future.

"I love you," she whispered. "I almost want to wait and see if you come back without Miss Rogers."

"Remember," he said, "a bird in the hand is worth two in the bush. And also, the doctor and you are a team. I've seen you both in action. I think you would be very happy together."

Alice nodded her head and then she turned and walked over to Clint's hotel door, shut and locked it.

"What are you doing?"

She began to unbutton her blouse. "One last time?"

The saddlebags slipped forgotten from Clint's hands and spilled their contents across the floor.

"What have I done?" he said in a voice already thick with desire.

She said, flying into his arms, "You've created a very passionate woman who has one hell of a lot of catching up to do."

NINE

Ian had been unequivocal when he'd told told Joanna that, if she was unable or unwilling to earn her five thousand dollars of "freedom" money on her back, that she must somehow do it on her feet. And now, as she stood waiting in the wings of the Bulldog Saloon's stage, Joanna was almost faint with fright.

"Here," Ian said, shoving a pint bottle of cherry-flavored liqueur in her face, "drink this. It will take care of the butterflies."

"No," she pleaded. "Ian, I'm not ready to perform!"

"You're not ready to pleasure a man, either. So get out there before I slap you to hell and back."

"Please, Ian!"

Sensing her terror, he softened his voice. "Listen, honey, in that new red dress, you could win their hearts if all you did was stand on stage and belch. Now drink a little bit of that stuff and get ready to put on a show!"

Joanna pressed the bottle to her lips. The liqueur was syrupy and sickeningly sweet but with Ian hovering over her, she had no choice but to drink. Gagging and choking, she managed to get four or five gulps down. It burned her throat.

"And now," the announcer on stage was saying,

"tonight we have a special treat for you, gentlemen. Miss Joanna Rogers will sing and dance!"

Through her teared eyes and the acrid blue smoke from Ian's cigar, Joanna heard the roomful of rough miners hoot, jeer and stomp their heavy work boots against the oak floor. It sounded like cattle stampeding across a wooden bridge. She clung to Ian's arm but he shoved her out, hissing, "Raise them skirts and bounce them tits and you'll be fine!"

Joanna almost tripped and fell as she reeled onto stage. At the mere sight of her low-cut dress that revealed most of her perspiring bosom, and with a hemline so immodest that it was only calf length, she caused the miners to gasp in startled appreciation.

Most of the women who performed in the mining towns were heavy, thick-legged and coarse. Joanna, with her blond hair piled over her head in soft, golden curls, was almost angelic in comparison.

A big, good-looking miner with a bottle in his right fist stood up and doffed his slouch hat. He bowed slightly and bellowed, "Miss Rogers, you just sing and jump around a little bit and when you're all tuckered out, little angel, I'll make sure that no one throws anything at you but cash."

The big man pivoted full around, his eyes challenging, his jaw jutting out aggressively. He was intimidating but no one paid him any attention because all eyes were on Joanna.

A man in a black bowler and wearing a red garter around his right bicep jammed his fingers at a dirty keyboard and the saloon's out-of-tune piano banged out a lively Comstock favorite called "Lucy from Louisiana." It was slightly bawdy and told the story of a little farm girl who was tricked by a drummer into coming to the Comstock. Lucy wound up being a "crib queen" up on A

THE DEADLY DERRINGER 73

Street and pining away for the love she'd never known.

Joanna's voice quavered from fear rather than feigned emotion as she clasped her hands and sang the last few lines of the tragedy.

> And poor Lucy from Louisiana,
> she fell so mighty low,
> and when she died on Sunday,
> all the boys put on a show.
> So if you ever find a farm girl
> alooking for a thrill,
> don't take her to the Comstock,
> or she'll wind up dead and still.

It was a stupid song that Joanna hated but everyone said she could sing and sing well. And with her blond curls, sad blue eyes and clenched hands over sweaty breasts, she made a tremendous impression. As the last sad words of the song died on her lips, more than one rough hard-rock miner wiped away a tear.

"Let's hear it for Miss Joanna Rogers!" the tall, handsome man shouted, pulling a wad of money from his pocket and hurling it at her.

A moment later, the crowd was on its feet, shouting and applauding and throwing money. Most of it was small change, but all together, it added up to a tidy sum.

Joanna turned to look at Ian standing in the wings, a wide grin on his face. He gave her a thumbs-up sign and she took courage and immediately broke into "Sweet Betsy from Pike." It was another favorite and the crowd loved it almost as well. Joanna's third song, however, proved to be the most popular of all. Kicking and dancing, she sang a song about a handsome young miner who fell in love with a governor's daughter and became a rich man.

The lyrics, like all the other songs, were pretty nonsensical, but with her kicks and bouncing bosom, nobody cared. When she was finished, the roar of applause filled the saloon and more coins showered her until the saloon's owner, fearing for Joanna's physical safety, came out and dragged her off stage.

"She'll be back in fifteen minutes!" he cried as men shouted for an encore.

Joanna, dazed and dumbfounded, found herself being crushed in a mighty bear hug by Ian.

"I knew you would do that to them!" he shouted. "Look at all that money out there! You're gonna make us a fortune!"

Joanna shook her head to clear her whirling thoughts. "No," she said. "Five thousand dollars. That's what you said and that's all I'll do."

The look of elation evaporated from his face. "Sure," he told her as he pushed her aside and hurried out to join the saloon owner in collecting the coins and bills that littered the stage.

Joanna almost turned and ran from him at that unguarded moment. But she didn't because, dressed in this outfit, how far could she really hope to run before he closed in and caught her? He'd already threatened to beat her to a bloody pulp if she ever tried to run away before she earned him five thousand. And if she sought help, Joanna knew that she would be giving some poor, well-meaning fool a veritable death sentence.

So she stayed in the wings and watched as the rough miners stomped their feet, drank, even linked arms and did jigs as they waited for her to return and perform.

Joanna supposed that she should have felt some jubilation about being such a hit on the stage. But she felt nothing but revulsion just now. Her dress was that of a cheap whore. And it was her *body*, not her voice or some small degree of stage talent, that had won the hearts of these crude miners. They had drooled to watch her sweat and bounce, and once stimulated, they'd probably rush out and visit the prostitutes up on A Street.

Joanna sighed and then whispered to herself, "Better them than me."

"Get ready, honey," Ian said, rushing up to her side. "We collected over six dollars out there!"

"I saw more than that!"

"Saloon gets half," Ian said quickly, as he looked away and waved to the heavyset saloon owner. "That's standard procedure."

"Since when?"

"Always has been."

Joanna's heart sank. What this meant was that she would have to earn ten thousand dollars in tips and wages before she was free of this man.

"I'll never be free of you," she said in a broken voice.

"Aw, sure you will! Now, come on, honey, buck up and show some life out there!"

Before Joanna could argue with him, she heard the piano player pounding on his keyboard again. They would do the same three songs again, over and over, because they were the only ones that she had rehearsed.

"Get out there!" Ian said, shoving her on stage again.

"Hey, sweetie," the big, handsome young man with the aggressive jaw shouted as he came to his feet, "how about a little kiss for your loudest supporter?"

Joanna swallowed, managed to shake her head and start to sing. She didn't know what was going to come of her life in the days, weeks and months to come, but she was looking for exactly the kind of big, strong young man out there now grinning at her to help her escape Ian's grasp. And if she warned him about the deadly hideout derringer, maybe he could survive and deliver her from this nightmarish existence.

Joanna forced a smile and even winked at the man who was bigger and stronger than Ian. The other miners howled with delight and the handsome man shoved his way to the stage and tried to grab and yank down the front of her dress.

The saloon owner and two of his bouncers appeared as from nowhere and one of them had a short truncheon of some kind. One minute the huge drunken miner was pawing at the front of her dress, the very next he was laid out cold on the floor and being dragged unceremoniously toward the back door.

Joanna glanced over her shoulder at Ian, who was grinning wickedly as if he'd read her secret thoughts of deliverance.

Damn him, Joanna raged as the piano player missed a key and she struggled to remember the sad end to her song.

Ten minutes later, she was being showered by money again and, this time, she did not allow Ian and the saloon owner to collect her homage. Down on her knees, oblivious to the fact that her breasts were spilling out for everyone in the audience to see, Joanna scooped up the money herself.

"We'll get the tips!" Ian spat after they returned to the wings.

"Not all of them, you won't," Joanna said. "If I let you do it, I'll *never* be free."

Ian, seeing her grim and determined expression, neither backhanded her nor even said a word in anger. He just forced a wintry smile and walked away.

TEN

The word spread rapidly in Virginia City about the beautiful new singer and dancer. Each night, Joanna sang to ever-larger crowds and added one new song. By the end of the first week, the love-starved miners were not only tossing money in her direction after each performance, but also flowers.

"They're paying five dollars for a single damn rose!" Ian stormed. "Tell them not to throw flowers but to stick to money."

"I can't do that," Joanna said. "And I won't do it."

Ian balled his fist but Joanna did not flinch as she would have in the past. "If you hit me in the face and I tell the crowd, they'll tear you limb from limb."

He grabbed her arm and twisted it up behind her back until she sobbed, "Stop, please!"

"What are you going to tell them about me doing this?"

"Nothing!"

He released her. "You're getting too big for your britches," he snarled. "You're beginning to think that, just because you're so popular with the miners, that you're big enough to tell me to go to hell. Well you're not! I'll kill you before I let you go."

Joanna looked up into his face. How could she once have thought him handsome? Now, all she could see was his cruel mouth, his black, pitiless eyes that mirrored a twisted, inhuman spirit. How could she have been so blind not see what kind of monster he truly was inside!

"I been thinking about us getting married, after all," he said quite suddenly. "I think we'll go ahead and get married. Maybe today."

She wiped her tear-streaked face. "I told you I'd never marry you."

"What you say don't mean a thing. If I say we marry, then we marry."

In Joanna's heart, she knew that he was right. She didn't have the courage to oppose him anymore. Ian almost never left her out of his sight, and then for only a few minutes. His gambling, which was the reason he'd come to the Comstock, had never gotten off the ground.

And why should it, she thought bitterly, when he can stand in the wings and then rush out on stage three or four times a night and make several hundred dollars without risking his life because of a deck of marked cards.

"You'll become Mrs. Ian Palmer. I'll give you my name and some respectability."

She glared at him. "If you expect gratitude, forget it. The only reason you've decided to marry me is that you don't want your gilded bird to fly the cage."

He leered at her. "We'll get married tomorrow afternoon, honey. I'll find a preacher and we'll do it up right. Maybe even have some cake and champagne. But no flowers. Save the ones that they throw tonight."

Joanna turned away but he grabbed her by the arm and spun her roughly about. He pulled her to his chest and ravaged her lips. "I ain't gettin' no virgin bride," he

THE DEADLY DERRINGER 79

said. "And I ain't waitin' for our wedding night. I'll give you another lesson in pleasin' a man tonight."

"I despise you," she whispered. "I'd almost be willing to die myself if it would hurt you."

He wound his fingers into her hair and he yanked back her head, exposing her throat which he sucked on until it hurt and there was a dark red mark to show that she belonged exclusively to him, body and soul.

"Let them see that on your neck when you go on stage tonight," he said. "Maybe that will cool their passion a little. They can just guess where I'll put other marks on that lovely body of yours when we go to bed."

Joanna turned away, feeling sick to her stomach. One way or another, she decided, she had to escape this man before he forced her to the altar. Once a woman took a husband, she had no rights of her own. Her property became that of her man and he could do damn near anything he wanted to her and no one would lift a hand.

Somehow, then, she would escape him tonight even if it meant that she might well die in the attempt.

Joanna was sick to her stomach all that early evening until her first show and even then was so nervous and upset that she could barely sing. To compensate, she bounced around on stage a little more than usual and bent over to let them peek down her dress more, too.

By midnight, she had been on stage three times and there was only one performance to go. After that, Ian would collect her tips and usher her back to their hotel room where he would ravish her. The hell would finally end about two in the morning when he fell asleep.

"No more," she vowed as she stood in the wings and tried over and over to come up with some clever way to elude Ian and escape his grasp.

"Get ready," he said. "And try and remember your lines a little better. I guess the thought of what I have in mind to do to you tonight has you a little flustered, huh?"

"It's made me want to throw up," she said just as the piano music started and she jumped out of this his reach to the raucous applause of the crowd.

But instead of singing, Joanna raised her hands for silence. She had not planned to do this, but now she knew that she would never come up with some clever escape and that her only hope was with the audience itself.

"My friends," she said, "I need your help. I'm being held in bondage by Ian Palmer, the man who comes out every night and collects all the money you throw. I haven't a cent to show for your generosity and Ian has vowed to kill me if I confess to you what he is doing. I *need* your help."

"Damn you!" Ian shouted as he started for her.

But the crowd, after a moment of stunned silence, came to its feet as one and surged toward the stage. Joanna felt a bullet strike her in the hip and she collapsed as more gunfire exploded from the wings. She thought that she saw a miner take a bullet in the stomach and go down, but she couldn't be sure as the enraged miners rushed Ian, who turned and fled.

"Are you all right?" a miner cried, trying to protect her from being trampled to death.

She gritted her teeth. "I'm going to be all right now, I think."

The miner was young but very strong. He had sand-colored hair, nice blue eyes and a soothing voice. He picked her up as if she weighed nothing. "Just hang on," he pleaded, "I'm going to rush you to a doctor!"

THE DEADLY DERRINGER 81

There was so much confusion and shouting that Joanna closed her eyes and laid her head against the man's chest. "Don't let him come back for me," she said, "please don't ever let him come back for me."

"Miss Rogers, he'll have to kill half the men on the Comstock to get to you again. I promise you he will."

Joanna managed a smile and when she was borne outside, she felt the cool, high-desert air on her cheeks, bare chest and legs. Very, very immodest, she thought.

"You're going to live," the young man said as other miners shouted for a way to be cleared to the doctor's office. "You're going to live to sing and dance again, Miss Rogers."

"I hope so," she told him and then she closed her eyes and drifted off into unconsciousness.

When a doctor came running up in his nightclothes to open his office, Joanna was rushed inside.

"Put her on that examining table and then get out of here," the doctor ordered, seeing the huge bloodstain on her dress.

"I'm staying," the young man vowed. "I won't look, but I won't go away, either. Not until that sonofabitch that shot her and one of my friends is dead."

The doctor did not have time to argue. He took Joanna's pulse with one hand, shoved her dress up above her hips with the other.

When he saw the wound, he swallowed and looked away for a moment. Seeing this, the young man was filled with alarm. "Isn't she going to live? What's wrong, Doc?"

The doctor took a better look before he said, "She'll live, all right. But the bullet shattered her pelvis. Her hip bone, if you will. She's the dancer and singer, isn't she?"

"Yeah, but . . ."

"Now she's just a singer," the doctor said quietly as he began to clean around the terrible wound before opening it up to dig out the bullet.

At his words, the young man's fists clenched at his sides. He turned away, ashamed at the tears that sprang unbidden to his eyes. To his mind, Joanna Rogers was an angel, or at least the closest thing to one he'd ever see in this world.

"What's your name, young man?"

"Randal," he said. "Quincy Randal."

"Well, Mr. Randal, if you've got any prayers, say one now. She's already lost a lot of blood and she's weak. She definitely won't dance again, so just pray that she'll live."

Quincy Randal did as the doctor asked. He bowed his head and prayed and prayed until he lost track of time.

"It's done," the doctor said.

Quincy turned to look and wished he hadn't. The doctor quickly began to bandage the wound. "She's going to live," he said. "I guess the Lord listened to your prayers."

"If he did, it was the first time."

The doctor finished bandaging. "Are you a good friend of this young woman?"

"No, sir. I . . . I don't think she had any friends. The man who shot her kept her to himself."

"I don't doubt that." The doctor sleeved sweat from his forehead. "She is a beautiful girl. Shame she has to make a living in a saloon."

"Maybe she won't have to now," Quincy said. "There's plenty of rich men who'd marry her whether she can dance or not."

"I'd like to think you're right," the doctor said. "Because she's going to need a lot of care and kindness before she will walk again."

Quincy raised his chin. "Until she finds a man with money, I got plenty of both."

"Yes," the doctor said. "I can see that very clearly despite the lateness of the hour."

For some reason, Quincy grinned his boyish smile. Miss Rogers was going to be all right. It didn't matter if an angel couldn't dance. It didn't matter at all.

ELEVEN

On the way to the Comstock Lode, Clint also visited the desert stage station.

"Hell, yes, I remember that mean sonofabitch! He damn near murdered me!"

"How long has it been since they passed through?"

"Couple weeks. Maybe longer." The station tender squinted his eyes. "You fixin' to spend the night? Give you a bed and a good feed for a dollar. Maybe throw in my squaw for an extra two bits."

"No, thanks." Clint dismounted. "I'll just have some water for me and my horse."

"Cost you two bits."

Clint frowned. "All right."

"Each."

The Gunsmith was not a man who liked being squeezed. True, the well belonged to this man, or his employer, and therefore some compensation for the effort was reasonable. But a half-dollar to quench his thirst and that of his black gelding, Duke, seemed entirely unreasonable.

"Two bits is more than enough for the both of us," Clint said, digging into his pocket for change and tossing it at the man's feet.

The station master blustered. "Dammit, you can just ride on if you ain't willn' to pay what's asked."

"Mister, you're not only greedy, but you're a fool. Take what I've offered and get out of my sight before my patience wears thin."

The man wheeled around and stomped off toward the station while Clint led his horse around back to the corral. He removed his Stetson and drank side by side with his horse. The water was sweet and the day was hot.

Duke heard the station master first and swung his head around. Clint, catching the warning, also whirled just in time to see the man start to raise a rifle to his shoulder.

The Gunmsmith's right hand flashed to the Colt strapped to his side and as he was lifting the pistol, he cocked it. The moment it cleared leather, the Colt was aimed and Clint fired. The entire sequence did not take a full second.

Clint's bullet smashed into the station tender's rifle and then glanced off the breech and struck the man's ribs.

The station tender howled and the impact of the bullet knocked him up against the station wall. Before Clint could decide what to do next, the man bolted into the sage and took off running for his life.

"Damn fool!" Clint swore, grabbing up his reins and swinging into his saddle. The smart thing to do was just to ride on. But if the station tender ran until he bled to death, Clint would be the one responsible for his death and suffering.

So he touched spurs to his horse and went galloping after the crazy man, overtaking him in less than a quarter mile.

"You'd better stop and let me take a look at that!"

"Get away from me!"

Clint had a rope and though he was not expert with it like a real cowboy, there had been times when he'd seen fit to toss a loop. This seemed like another one of those times. Untying his rope and then shaking out a loop, Clint whirled the rope overhead three or four times and managed to bring the man up short.

The Gunsmith tied the rope around his saddlehorn and dismounted. "Mister," he said, "I don't know if you're loco or what, but I'm going to take a look at that wound and then get you back to your station. After that, you can live or die and I don't care."

The man cursed and rushed him but with his arms pinioned at his sides by the rope, he was easy to knock down. Clint jumped on him, then yanked up his shirt and examined the ribs.

"You'll live," he said, tearing the man's shirt from his body and then ripping it into shreds for a bandage.

It took Clint ten minutes to get the bleeding stopped. That accomplished, he dragged the man to his feet and climbed back on his horse.

"One last question," Clint growled, hand moving over to rest on the butt of his gun. "How did the girl look?"

The station tender threw back his head and laughed, a high, crazy kind of laugh that made the hairs on the back of Clint's neck stand up tall.

"What's so damned funny?"

"Was she your woman?"

"Maybe."

"He screwed her in the dirt! We saw him doin' it right there in my corral!"

The man bent over double and laughed even harder despite a pretty nasty bullet wound. Clint shook his head and reined his horse toward the Comstock. The hell with taking this crazy, ornery old man back to his station. He could get there himself or he could just laugh himself to death. Clint didn't much care.

When he finally arrived on the Comstock Lode, the first thing he did was to visit the sheriff, a tough, competent-looking man in his late twenties named Frank Ross.

"So," Ross said, extending his hand and studying Clint with keen interest, "you're the Gunsmith."

"That's right." Clint measured Ross and found the man to his liking. They were about the same build and height. "Sheriff, you must be a pretty good man to keep a lid on this powder keg."

Ross released Clint's hand. "Have a chair. Can I get you a cup of coffee from the café next door?"

"No, thanks."

"A drink of whiskey?" Ross said, opening a drawer and pulling out a bottle and a glass.

"Sure."

Ross poured a generous two fingers and handed the glass to Clint. "I never drink when I'm working. Don't drink much at any time. As you well know, a sheriff is always on duty."

"Yep, I sure do," Clint said, taking a swallow to cut the dust after a long, hard trail. "That's why I handed over my badge and settled for a more peaceful life."

"If I were smart," Ross said, leaning back in his office chair and lacing his blunt fingers behind his head, "I'd do exactly the same. But I tried to once and I missed the excitement."

"I miss it too, for about a minute a year," Clint said with a wink and a smile.

"So," Ross said, "what brings you to Virginia City?"

Clint's smile died. "I'm looking for a very pretty and innocent young woman who made a very bad mistake by choosing the wrong kind of man."

THE DEADLY DERRINGER 89

"That happens all too often. And you think this girl came to my town?"

"I'm almost sure of it," Clint said. "Her name is Joanna Rogers and she was traveling with . . ."

"A murderin' sonofabitch named Ian Palmer," Ross said before Clint could finish. "Yeah, they were here. The young woman still is."

"Where?"

"She's at Mrs. Carry's house, shot in the hip by her boyfriend."

Clint swallowed. "Is she going to live?"

"Live, yes. But the doctor says she'll never walk again without a limp."

Clint groaned.

"The whole town is upset. Miss Rogers, you see, became quite a celebrity in the few weeks she danced and sang at one of the saloons."

"I'm surprised she'd do that."

"She was forced to by Palmer. But anyway, after she was shot, the town took up a collection to pay her bills. Must have raised a couple thousand dollars."

"I'm glad to hear it."

Ross leaned forward. "Miss Rogers practically has a waiting line to visit her every day. She isn't wasting away for company."

"I'll bet."

"Gunsmith, are you in love with her?"

Clint smiled. "I don't know. I can't even remember what she looks like."

Ross's eyebrows shot up. "I'm sure not calling you a liar, but she's got a face and figure that would tend to stick in a fella's memory."

Clint quickly explained how he'd been shot and had lost part of his memory. "I'm hoping to get it all back as time goes along," he ended up saying.

"Could be dangerous with as many enemies as you must have made over the years."

"Yes," Clint said. "It could be downright fatal."

Clint pushed himself to his feet. "Now, Sheriff, if you'll give me directions, I'll go see her when I leave. Where is Palmer?"

"I don't know," the sheriff said. "He shot the girl on stage, then killed another man and wounded several others before he dashed away in the night. We searched every building in this town and we never found a trace of him. If we had, there was nothing I could of done to keep the crowd from lynching him on the spot. They were that incensed by the shootings."

This time, the Gunsmith did swear. "Damnation! Did you check to see if anyone saw him in Reno, Carson City or somewhere else in these parts?"

Ross nodded. "I spent three days of hard riding. I damn near made a circle around the entire Comstock but no one has reported seeing the man. I think he's long gone. I sent in a description to the United States Territorial Marshal's office. They'll send an artist over and we'll have a wanted poster made up and circulated all over the West. But you know Palmer will either leave this country or change his name and appearance."

"Yeah," Clint said bitterly, "I know. Unless someone makes it their mission to hunt this man down, he'll never be apprehended."

"Are you going after him?"

"I am," Clint said. "First for Miss Rogers, then for myself and finally for all the other good men he's no doubt shot with that hideout derringer he carries hidden up his sleeve."

THE DEADLY DERRINGER 91

"Oh, yeah," Ross said, "Miss Rogers told me about that. She said that she had a good chance to look at it while they were living together. I understand it is adapted from the Kepplinger Holdout."

"The what?"

"It's a device invented by a man named Kepplinger so that, by moving his foot and rigging himself up with cables and pulleys, he could cause a spring-loaded sneak to slap a card into his palm. It was a damned ingenious device."

"I can imagine so," Clint said. "But the device that puts a derringer into Ian Palmer's hand isn't activated by his foot. Apparently, it's activated merely by him lifting his right hand and extending it as if to point."

"I see," Ross said. "That's a good piece of information to know. I guess it must be pretty foolproof and very, very fast."

"Yes," Clint said, thinking about how Palmer had caught him by surprise and gunned him down with both barrels of that derringer, "it's faster than anything I've ever seen."

Ross looked at him a bit strangely as if reading his mind but Clint did not elaborate as he finished his whiskey.

"I'd appreciate it if you'd let me know if you hear anything more about Palmer's whereabouts."

"You bet I will."

Clint shook the man's hand again, received directions on how to find the Carry house, then departed.

He was not looking forward to seeing Miss Rogers with a bullet-shattered hip, but see her he would. And then, he would set about taking up the trail of Ian Palmer. Someone, somewhere, had to have seen him flee Virginia City. It was just a matter of asking enough people before he found the right answer.

TWELVE

The Carry House was down on E Street, not far from the V. & T. Railroad Station. It was modest in size, but presented a neat appearance and there were red climbing roses on the picket fence and a small dog growling and barking behind it.

"Take it easy, boy," Clint said to the dog as he tied his horse up to the fence and went over to open the gate.

The dog, a brown and white cur with an underslung jaw and crooked teeth, attacked in a rush. It clamped its fangs onto Clint's boot top, and although it could not have weighed twenty pounds, it gave every evidence of its intention to rip the boot leather to shreds.

Clint glanced across the yard toward the house. He could see no one watching through the window so he booted the dog hard in the snout with his free leg and, when it still didn't let go, he kicked it harder, sending it flying into the roses. Cut by thorns, the little devil howled and took off running around the house.

"What is going on out here?" Mrs. Carry demanded, seeing just the back end of her vanishing mongrel.

Clint looked down at his torn pants. It was a good thing that the leather was thick on his boot tops or the dog would have chewed his leg up pretty good.

"That your little brown-and-white dog?"

"Of course it is! Why else would he be in my yard?"

Mrs. Carry was big, stout, and her hands were on her hips. She was probably only thirty but looked forty. It was obvious that frontier and mining-camp life had not been easy for her.

"Who are you?"

"My name is Clint Adams."

"If you came to see Miss Rogers, she's taking a nap. I'll tell you what I already told all the others. There are visiting hours and they're from five to six every afternoon and from noon to two on Sunday."

"I'm an old friend," Clint said, advancing a few steps before halting. "And I know she'd want to see me the minute I arrived in town."

"Come back at five o'clock and get in line," she said, unimpressed.

Clint could not see a way to get by this stubborn woman so he started to turn around and leave, but just then he heard Joanna's sweet voice calling his name from inside.

"Hear that? She wants to see me now," he said, brushing past Mrs. Carry and hurrying up the path to her door before going inside.

Clint followed the sound of Joanna's voice into a bedroom where he found her.

"Oh, Clint!" she cried happily. "I never thought I'd see you again!"

He hurried to her side and carefully sat down on her bed, then took her hand. "You look wonderful," he said, lying because she looked thin and pinched with pain.

She fought back tears. "Everything you said about Ian was right. He was a terrible man."

"Everyone gets fooled once in a while."

"Ian was a killer, Clint. He shot a freighter to death just outside of Dayton who wanted to help me. I had to help pull the man's body into the brush. And then he killed at least one man after he shot me."

"So I heard. He's got some kind of a device up his sleeve that slaps a hideout derringer into his palm faster than the blink of an eye. He used it on me, too."

Joanna reached out and Clint held her as she cried softly. "It's all right. He's gone and you've made a lot of friends here, Joanna. You can stay or I'll see that you get back to Candelaria."

Sniffling, she pushed away and looked into his eyes. "The doctor says that I won't be able to walk without a bad limp."

"Maybe not so bad," Clint said. "I've seen more than one man shot in the hip recover so completely that you could not even tell they'd had their hip shattered."

Joanna brightened. "Really?"

"Yes."

Taking a deep breath and expelling it slowly, Joanna said, "I want to stay here for a while. It's a rough town, but Candelaria is even worse and I've managed to make some dear friends since I've been here, despite Ian."

"Do you have any idea where he's gone?"

"No. Sheriff Ross has asked me that same question again and again."

"Ian never said a word about where he came from or anything of his past?"

Joanna frowned. "He did say something about Bodie, once. There's a town by that name, isn't there?"

"Yes."

"Well, more than once he said something about having friends there. It's really the only place he ever mentioned other than Virginia City."

"Did he have any good friends here that I could talk to?"

"No. He was friendly with Mr. Wolfe, the man who owns the Bulldog Saloon where I was forced to sing and dance. But other than him, I don't think Ian was on friendly terms with anyone. He rarely let me out of his sight."

More tears formed in Joanna's eyes. "I was like his slave," she said. "He could do about anything he wanted with me and I was almost helpless."

"Try to put it out of your mind," Clint said. "It wasn't your fault."

"Yes, it was! I was stupid not to take your warning more seriously. I thought I loved him and while I saw a few faults, I thought I could make them go away."

"You can't," Clint said. "A man almost never changes for a woman. If you want a good man, you've got to find one, not figure on creating one out of your own good intentions."

"I know that now."

Clint heard a noise in the hallway and twisted around to see Mrs. Carry holding her little dog, which was scratched up pretty good and whimpering pitifully.

"You threw little Boris into the roses, didn't you?" Mrs. Carry shouted.

"No, ma'am. He just sort of wanted to take a ride on my boot and I guess he landed where he shouldn't have."

"You *kicked* him into the roses!"

"That's not what I said."

"Get out of my house!" Mrs. Carry cried. "Get out and don't you ever come back."

"If he goes, then I'm going with him!" Joanna stormed.

THE DEADLY DERRINGER 97

"That's fine with me!"

"Now, Joanna," Clint said. "Maybe you ought to stay here. I'm riding after Ian and I'll find him no matter where he goes. When I've found and either arrested or killed him, then I'll come back for you. You'll be fit to travel by then."

Joanna squeezed Clint's hand. "Will you really come back for me?"

"I promise I will."

She believed him. "All right."

Clint stood up and put his hat on, but not before he bent and gave Joanna a kiss on her lips. As he turned and walked out the door, Mrs. Carry glared at him with angry eyes, and Boris, in the protection of his mistress's flabby arms, growled bravely.

"Little mongrel mutt," Clint muttered as he passed out of the bedroom and down the hall.

Just as he was reaching the front gate, Mrs. Carry released Boris, who came flying out of the house, growling and acting as if he would tear Clint apart. Clint glanced back, stepped through the gate and slammed it into Boris's ugly little snout.

The dog howled, reversed directions and went flying back into the house yip-yipping all the way. Clint could not hide a small, self-satisfied grin as he remounted Duke and rode back up to C Street to talk to the owner of the Bulldog Saloon.

"He wasn't no friend of mine," Howard Wolfe said in a gruff voice. "We just had a business arrangement together."

"So I heard," Clint said, not liking the fat, surly saloon owner. "You and Ian split most of the tips that Miss Rogers earned."

"I don't see that that's any of your business," Wolfe growled from behind the long, polished bar.

"I guess it isn't," Clint said. "But it is my business to find and either arrest or kill Ian Palmer. He's a wanted man and if you can help me, do it right now."

Wolfe shook his head. "I don't do anything except for money."

Clint took the saloon owner's measure. Wolfe was a hard man. He'd probably started out in life with nothing and now he owned a prosperous business. The kind of man who could reach that level of success was not going to be intimidated by mere words.

Clint reached into his pocket and pulled out several crumpled dollars. "I'm a little low on funds right now but you can have this money just for giving me a name."

Wolfe snorted with disgust. "Mister, I won't give you directions to the nearest outhouse for that kind of money. Now get out of here!"

When Wolfe started to turn his back and walk away, Clint grabbed the man by the wrist and smashed it down against the lip of his beer glass. The glass shattered and Wolfe cried out in pain. His cuff turned bright red and Clint knew that he'd cut a vein, maybe even an artery.

"Let go of me!" the man screamed. "I'm bleeding to death!"

"Yeah," the Gunsmith said, keeping an iron grip on the man's wrist. "I can see that. Be a shame to mess up this place with so much blood. I guess you probably ought to tell me where Ian Palmer might have gone before you lose any more blood."

"I don't know! He used to talk about how nice it was up at Lake Tahoe in the heat of the summer. Maybe he went up there!"

"He ever mention Bodie?"

"Yeah, once. Now let me go!"

Clint released the man and turned on his heel. Wolfe shot around the end of his bar and almost took his own batwing saloon doors with him as he burst outside and went racing toward the nearest doctor's office.

The Gunsmith went to his horse and mounted with a thoughtful expression. Before he reined away from the hitch rail, he extracted one of the few coins left in his pocket and tossed it end over end into the air.

"Heads we start looking at Lake Tahoe, tails we ride back down to Bodie."

It was tails. Clint was mildly disappointed because he'd heard Bodie was an awful place—hotter than blazes in summer, snow and ice in winter. It was also without law and considered to be a haven for the worst cutthroats imaginable. And since the Gunsmith was so well known throughout the West, it would not be surprising if he were recognized by a few of his old enemies, men he'd either sent to prison, or who had brothers or fathers he'd killed or captured.

Clint put his coin away. "Bodie, then," he said, not having a good feeling about the coin toss but superstitious enough to believe it would be even worse luck to ignore it and go first to Lake Tahoe.

THIRTEEN

On his way down to Bodie, Clint had stopped at another stage station where three men were sweating and cursing a they tried to repair a broken wagon wheel.

"Mind if I water my horse?"

"Help yourself," one of them grunted without even bothering to look up.

Clint went to the water trough but Duke, after taking a short gulp, refused to drink. Clint cupped a swallow and took a sip. It was awful and he spit it out.

"You drink this stuff?" he asked.

The man in charge looked up again. "Damn right. A man can't drink nothing but beer and whiskey, unless he's rich."

"Tastes like poison to me," Clint said, removing his Stetson and mopping his damp brow.

"Yeah," the man said, "but a body either survives and gets used to it, or else."

Clint did not have to ask what the "or else" was supposed to mean. "Need some help?"

"You a wheelwright?"

"Nope."

"Good at a forge?"

"Nope."

"Then you wouldn't be any help," the man said as he worked over the wheel.

"How far to Bodie?"

"Only about twenty-five miles. But if you're looking for sweet water, you won't find any there, either."

"Say," another one of the men grunted, "ain't you the Gunsmith?"

Clint sighed. "I've been called that."

"Hell, yes, you have! I saw you face off against the Mantee brothers over in El Paso. They damn near had that town buffaloed until you showed up. Even with your reputation, the odds were still running three to one that you'd get shot before you could drop both them brothers."

All three of the men were staring at Clint now with sudden interest. The first man who'd spoken, the one Clint judged to be the boss, said, "I'd heard that you were gunned down in Candelaria about a month ago. I should have known that it wasn't true."

"It was true," Clint admitted. "And that's why I'm hunting the man that laid me low. His name is Ian Palmer. Ever hear of him?"

All three shook their heads and the boss wiped his hands on his pants to clean them, then came over and offered to shake. "My name is Ben Wilson, that's Dade Catlow and Charley Benson. So what does this Palmer fella look like?"

Clint described him. "He's a real dandy. You'd spot him in a minute as a gambler."

"What kind of a horse do you figure he was riding?"

Clint had asked that same question in Virginia City and he had come up empty. "He shot a young woman and a miner at the Bulldog Saloon and took off on the run. No one saw him steal a horse so he might even have

THE DEADLY DERRINGER 103

jumped into the back of a passing wagon. I just don't know if he's riding a horse or if he came through on a wagon or stage."

"Most likely," Benson said, "he'd change his name. Maybe even grow a beard."

"I know that," Clint said, "but I'm told he had friends in Bodie and there might be too many people who knew his true identity to change his name. At least, that's what I'm counting on."

"He got any kinfolk around?" Wilson asked.

"Not that I know of."

Wilson shook his head. "Sounds to me like you're runnin' long odds of finding him."

"I'll find him, all right," Clint said. "I won't stop hunting until he's either dead, or swinging from a rope."

"We hear of such a man, we'll try and get word to you," Wilson offered.

Clint remounted. "I'd be obliged."

He started to ride on but Wilson said, "Is it true that you caught Bill Vacca and shot one of his brothers over in Arizona Territory?"

"Yeah. Bill was like a mad dog. He'd killed no less than three men when I finally stopped him. I tried to arrest the man, but he knew he'd hang so he went for his gun."

"I guess I'd do the same," Wilson said. "Better to go down fighting than kicking at the end of a rope."

"Bill thought so."

"What'd his kid brother do to get hisself shot?"

"He tried to ambush me a couple of days later. I got lucky. His horse was a mare in heat. She whinnied when she smelled my gelding."

"Fine-looking animal, there."

"Thanks, but he's mighty thirsty for some good water," Clint said.

"I got some in a keg that they haul in from the Walker River. We'll give him his fill."

"Maybe I better go to Bodie. I haven't got but a couple of dollars to my name."

"Hell," Wilson said, forgetting the wagon wheel for the moment. "Who said anything about money?"

Ten minutes later, Clint was back in the saddle and Wilson and his men were standing around close. Wilson shook the Gunsmith's hand again and said, "You remember me asking about Bill Vacca and his brother?"

"Sure."

"Well, I had a reason."

"What reason?"

"There's a passel of men in Bodie by the name of Vacca. Big, tall, lanky bastards. Rougher than cobs. Might be they're kin of Bill and his kid brother. Might be that once they hear you're in town, they'll come looking to gun you down."

"I was afraid I might generate that kind of a reception," Clint said. "But there's not much help for it."

"There's at least five of 'em," Dade Catlow, the quietest of the three, offered. "I seen 'em plenty. They're mean and they're bullies. You wouldn't want to cross men like that."

"I don't intend to cross them," Clint said. "But I won't shy away from visiting Bodie in order to find Ian Palmer."

"But you said yourself that you didn't even know if he was there."

"That's right." Clint pulled his Stetson down low over his eyes. "However, I'll know by this time tomorrow. Any other enemies I might have waiting in Bodie?"

"There's old Jessie Lane," Benson said. "I'd guess you've heard of him."

"I have," Clint said, remembering the man's face on many a wanted poster. "He was a highwayman for many years. Pretty good with a gun, too."

"Well, he's in town."

"Doing what?"

"Gambling and drinking. I hear that he's running one of the saloons and he's got a few men working for him that cheat pretty good at the card tables."

"Sounds like a leopard that never changed his spots," Clint said.

"You ever bring him into justice?"

"Twice. Once over near San Antonio, then a second time in Santa Fe."

"Well, then you'd better watch out for old Jessie. He's the kind of man who'd set his men on you in the dark. Maybe ambush you from an alley."

Clint shook his head. "Sounds like Bodie is living up to its reputation as being one of the hellholes of the West."

"That's right," Wilson said. "They got two undertakers and I heard that they're busy every single day. That's one of the reasons why we live and work right here. A man don't need to take any more chances than is necessary."

"Amen," Clint said. "I don't understand why the law-abiding people of Bodie don't hire themselves a good man and clean up their town."

The men exchanged questioning glances and then Wilson said, "Only a man with a death wish would put on a badge in Bodie. Besides, I don't guess there are enough decent men there that want the town cleaned up."

"You might be surprised," Clint said. "What I've come to discover is that there are usually enough good people but they're often afraid to stand up and speak out. If they did and no one backed them, they'd either be shot or run out of town."

"Maybe you'd like to take on that job," Dade Catlow said, studying Clint with real interest.

"Nope." Clint offered Catlow a half-smile. "The world has enough fools already. All I want is Ian Palmer. He's the one that I've got a score to settle with."

"Maybe so," Catlow said, "but I'll bet the Vacca brothers and old Jessie have a score to settle with you."

"If so, I guess I'll be easy enough to find."

"Could be interesting," Benson said. "You as fast with that six-gun as I've heard?"

"Probably not," Clint replied.

"Mind showing us?"

"Yeah," Clint said, "I do. You see, a long time ago I promised myself I'd never show off with a six-gun. That means that, when I draw it, I mean to shoot something that needs killing. But if I can beat a man before he even clears leather, then so much the better. That will usually convince him to submit to an arrest."

Benson nodded, but he looked discouraged. "I've just heard all my life about the really fast gunfighters. I never met one up close like you before. It would have been interesting."

"Come ride along with me to Bodie," Clint said with a wink. "You might see more shooting than you've stomach for."

Catlow and Wilson laughed at that and Clint reined his gelding south and rode on toward Bodie. He'd made a joke about what he might find in Bodie, but to him, the joke was not that funny.

FOURTEEN

It was nearly sunset when Clint topped a low, barren ridge and rode Duke down the dusty road into Bodie. He was surprised at the size of the town, but being a man who'd traveled widely across the West, his eyes missed almost nothing.

Bodie wasn't nearly as large or as prosperous as Virginia City, but it sure as the deuce qualified as being a major mining town. Clint recalled that Bodie's first gold discovery had taken place just before the Civil War and then the ore had gradually petered out until a few years ago. Still, judging from the size of the business district and the number of houses, tents, shacks and mine tailings, Clint was pretty sure that Bodie's population had to be at least ten thousand.

"A town that big ought to have some decent people wanting a little law and order," he said to himself.

Ten, hell, even five years ago, his heart would have quickened with the thought of cleaning up a lawless town like Bodie. Usually, a good man with a gun and plenty of guts could come into a place like this and earn himself maybe as much as a thousand dollars by restoring order. Clint had done it on several occasions. It was money well spent for the respectable citizens and businessmen who were often victims of extortion and worse.

Clint remembered a booming mining town called Wolf's Point in Montana. When he'd first arrived, the respectable citizens were on the verge of being run out of town. They'd pleaded with him, offered him to name his price if he'd only help them.

The price had been seven hundred dollars in advance and Clint had only needed to kill the baddest man in Wolf's Point to convince the other thugs, thiefs and murderers to leave town on the run. He'd been feted like a hero. The town's most successful madam, perhaps worried that he might even close her house down, had given him a free room for a week with all the girls he'd been able to handle.

What a fine time he'd had in Wolf's Point! He'd eaten the best food that the town had to offer, drank his fill of expensive imported wines and liquor, and loved himself half to death.

"But that was seven, maybe eight years ago and Wolf's Point sure wasn't any Bodie," he said to himself out loud. "I might have been a shade quicker on the gun then and I still had a lot of luck behind me. Things change. A man gets smarter or he gets killed."

Clint smiled and patted his horse's muscular neck as he rode on down toward Bodie. "But it sure was a grand time I had, Duke. And I'll just bet, if I wasn't in such a hurry to catch Ian Palmer, that I'm still man enough to tame a town like this one."

In reply, Duke flicked his ears back and forth and, perhaps sensing that the long ride was over and he was about to be rewarded with a good feed and clean stall, he quickened his pace.

By the time that Clint arrived in Bodie, the sun was

THE DEADLY DERRINGER 109

just going down over the distant Sierras far to the west. Bodie rested in an arid bowl surrounded by rocky hills. There appeared to be very few trees, and no doubt every drop of water that the town used was imported. Either that, or there were a couple deep wells that fed Bodie its life-giving water.

Clint was rather grateful for the gathering darkness that would allow him to enter Bodie without being recognized. He found a livery stable on the east end of the main street and dismounted feeling weary. His head was throbbing somewhat and he needed to take some of the headache powders that Dr. Mead had given him for just this kind of problem.

An old man, bent with a hard lean to the left, appeared from his office. He dismissed the Gunsmith in a glance as his eyes rested on Duke. "Damn fine-looking animal," he said, "though way too thin."

"He's been on the trail for almost a week now," Clint said. "This time of year, the feed isn't the best out there in the hills."

"An animal like that needs to be grained heavy," the man said, stroking Duke's flanks. "Needs to be curried and his shoes want for replacing."

"Already?"

The old man bent even lower and stuck the corncob pipe whose stem he was chewing into his coat pocket before he took Duke's right front fetlock in his hands. "Lookee here, mister. See how his hoof is pullin' free of them nails because it's growed so long? Why, I wouldn't be surprised if he didn't go lame in another fifteen or twenty miles."

"I suppose you've got a good blacksmith in mind?"

"Me. Abe Timber. I been shoeing good and bad horses for more'n fifty years. Ain't no one better at it."

"How much?"

"Ten dollars."

"Last time I had Duke shod I only paid five."

Timber dropped Duke's hoof and straightened as much as he could. "Five dollars! Why, I was gettin' five dollars ten years ago! Besides, here in Bodie, everything costs double, so you see, ten dollars is about fair."

"I'll pay you eight if I win at cards."

Timber shook his head. "I heard that a thousand times and it never put food on my table. You want your horse fed, curried and grained, it's cash in advance."

"I've only got two dollars to my name."

"Sell me your horse."

"Never," Clint said, reaching into his saddlebags and bringing out a spare six-gun. "What will you give me for this?"

Abe took it over to a lantern and even though his fingers were bent and thick from too many years of hard work, he handled the gun with surprising ease.

"Nice weapon, once."

Clint hid a smile. "It's *still* a nice pistol. I ought to know, I'm a gunsmith by trade. You were right about my horse needing shoes, I'm right about that six-shooter. I need . . . thirty dollars."

"Ha!"

"Twenty-five then."

"Twenty," Timber grunted.

"If you throw in a night's feed bill and a set of new shoes for my horse."

"Feed bill, okay, but five dollars extra for the horse shoes."

If his head hadn't been pounding, Clint would have haggled awhile and tried to wear the old man down. But his head was pounding and he was tired and hungry. "It's a deal."

Timber smacked his callused old palms together and nodded his head. He stuck the six-gun behind his belt and dug into his pockets for the cash.

"What's your handle?"

"Clint. Where's the best place to eat and get a room?"

"Eat at Potter's Café just up the street. As for a room, you can pay a dollar at the Celestial Hotel, or two dollars at the Governor's House. Or, you can sleep in my hay loft for two bits."

"Thanks," Clint said, unbuckling his saddlebags. "I'll think about it after supper."

As Clint was walking out the door, the man called, "Hey, mister!"

"Yeah?" Clint asked as he turned around.

"Haven't I seen you someplace before?"

"I don't know. Maybe."

"Seems to me I've seen you . . . or maybe your picture someplace."

"No matter," Clint said, walking away.

Potter's Café was good. Clint had a thick steak, a mound of fried potatoes, three cups of strong coffee and a quarter of an apple pie for dessert. The only unpleasant part of the experience was paying the bill, which came to just over two dollars.

"That's more than most cowboys make in a day," he complained.

"There ain't no cowboys in this country," the cashier told him. "And if you don't like the prices, you can find cheaper."

Clint growled a reply and went outside. In truth, he guessed everything in this town was probably damned expensive. Like Virginia City, nothing could be grown nearby and so all food and drink had to be imported. Freighting was expensive and no one was in business to lose money.

Clint rubbed a three-day-old stubble of beard. He looked hard-used but then, so did most everyone in this town. He considered the choices for a room and decided that he'd earned the best that Bodie had to offer. Besides, the Governor's House was just half a block down the street.

Clint paid the hotel clerk, receiving a bath for the price he was being charged. An hour later, he was clean-shaven, scrubbed, and pulling on a fresh pair of pants and shirt. Studying himself in the mirror, he supposed he would pass for a man of some means, though he was certainly not what anyone would consider well dressed.

The Gunsmith counted his money, reckoned he could afford to gamble with ten dollars and stuffed the rest in his boots before pulling them on and heading off to find a poker game where he could sit with his back to a wall and survey everyone who came or went while he was playing cards.

He remembered Jessie Lane's ugly face and Clint supposed the Vacca brothers would bear a strong enough resemblance to Bill and their ambushing kid brother that he would recognize them, too. As for Ian Palmer, well, he was going to ask some questions. If Palmer was in Bodie, Clint wanted to find him right sudden, either arrest or kill him, and get out of this town quickly.

It did not take long to discover that finding a saloon with a game was the easiest thing imaginable in Bodie. Given the town's size, it was remarkable how many saloons there were, and they were all filled with loud, mostly drunk miners with the money and orneriness to blow off steam.

THE DEADLY DERRINGER 113

In the space of twenty minutes, Clint found the kind of poker game that he liked. The players were a good mix, some miners who fumbled with cards, drank too much and would lose their wages long before midnight, a pair of professionals like himself, and one rather nervous young man in a black suit who was so tightfisted he had to be prodded even to tender his two-bit ante.

"Seven-card draw," a miner said, fumbling with the deck and making a poor show of shuffling and then dealing the cards.

For the first half-hour, Clint played to minimize his losses because the cards were not in his favor. In that time, he kept one eye on the door and the room and his other eye on the players, sizing each up and reaching a conclusion as to which of the players were going to be good enough to pose him problems.

Clint dismissed the miners and the tightfisted man immediately and one of the men he'd thought was a card sharp turned out to be reckless and impulsive. That left a man who referred to himself as Mr. Meeks.

"Mr. Meeks will call the bet and raise a dollar," he would say as if Mr. Meeks was someone other than himself. Or, "Mr. Meeks will have two cards, please."

Clint found the habit extremely annoying and it did not help that Mr. Meeks soon proved to be an expert gambler. He was a frail, even tubercular-looking man, impeccably dressed and with long, pale and manicured fingers. It was obvious that the man had never suffered hard labor, or any kind of labor, for that matter. Meeks had the look of someone who had detached himself entirely from life's cares. He smiled often, smoked prerolled French cigarettes that he took from a silver case and seemed entirely too pleasant to be living in a raw frontier town.

Clint could not quite figure the man out for a good long

while. Meeks was winning steadily, more than himself, and so charming that the losers did not even seem to begrudge their losses. But after an hour of playing, Clint detected the man dealing from the bottom of the deck. He thought at first that his eyes might be betraying him but then, about a quarter of an hour later, he saw it happen again.

Clint said nothing during the next two hours while miners came and went, all losing their money. In the meantime, Clint continued winning and with this newfound knowledge he now had a distinct edge, for he would not bet when Meeks was dealing.

By midnight, however, he was tired of the game. So far, he had not seen the Vacca brothers or received any news of Ian Palmer after asking each new player.

"Is this Mr. Palmer an old friend," Meeks said, "or perhaps an enemy?"

"An enemy."

Meeks studied his hand before his soft brown eyes met Clint's and he said, "And if this Mr. Palmer should walk though the door behind me, would you open fire, perhaps endangering Mr. Meeks's life?"

"I would not just open fire and take the chance that a stray bullet would hit you."

"How can Mr. Meeks believe this?"

"He can because I always hit what I aim for," Clint said.

Meeks thought about this for almost a quarter of an hour. He was winning steadily, accumulating quite a pile of chips and no doubt would have preferred to remain where he was if Clint had not been across the table from him and ready to draw his gun at any moment.

"Mr. Meeks has decided to retire after dealing this hand, gentlemen," he said, referring only to Clint.

THE DEADLY DERRINGER 115

There was some grumbling because no one liked the table's winner to quit but it was the man's right to do so and Meeks could not be denied.

Meeks dealt the cards and Clint drew a pair of jacks. He called for two more cards and was disappointed to wind up with nothing better than an additional pair of threes.

Meeks was watching the Gunsmith very closely now. "Mr. Meeks will take two cards."

Clint knew that Meeks was going to deal himself off the bottom of the deck.

"Put the deck on the table," he said, "and then take the cards off one by one."

Meeks froze like a wax statue. His eyes grew hard and his voice changed, deepening in timbre. "Mr. Meeks does not understand your request, sir."

"Sure, you do." It was Clint's turn to smile. "Just put them on the table and take the top two cards."

Meeks swallowed. "This is highly irregular. Insulting, even."

"I don't care," Clint said. "Better to be insulted and live, than to take the insult foolishly and perhaps die. Eh, Meeks?"

The man really began to sweat when Clint said, "Let's just make this the last hand for us. Your stack of chips against mine. How about it?"

"My stack is twice your stack! Why should I agree?"

"You know why. Should I tell the others?"

"What the hell is going on here?" a player who was glassy-eyed from whiskey demanded.

Clint ignored the man and pushed out his chips. "Take your cards and I call."

Meeks had a hideout gun, Clint was sure of it, and equally sure that the mild little man was deadly. So Clint said, "I wonder if Mr. Meeks knows that he is about to die if he does what he is considering?"

Meeks made the correct decision after looking deep into the Gunsmith's eyes and finding no weakness or bluff. He carefully laid the deck face down on the table and slipped off the top two cards.

"Anyone else willing to bet against our stacks of chips?" Clint asked around the table.

No one said a word.

"All right, Mr. Meeks, what do you have?"

"Nothing, goddamn you," the man hissed.

"Then I think Mr. Meeks is through for tonight," Clint said, raking the man's pile of chips into his lap and waiting to see if he would lose his composure and go for his hideout gun.

But Meeks forced a brittle smile and pushed back into his chair and unwound slowly to his feet. He was very thin. "If I meet Mr. Ian Palmer, I will certainly tell him to aim for your balls, sir," he said, "for they are much, much too large."

Clint studied the man. "If I see you cheating again, you had better either use that gun up your sleeve, or leave Bodie. Is that understood?"

A blue vein throbbed visibly in the man's forehead and then he stiffly turned and walked away.

"What the hell was that all about?" the drunken miner demanded. "Was he cheatin', or what?"

Clint stood up and raked his chips and those of Mr. Meeks into his Stetson. "I don't know," he said offhandedly, "I guess it's possible."

And then, with the entire saloon staring at him, he cashed in his winnings and headed out the door. He would spend the next hour or two visiting the other saloons seeking Ian Palmer. And then he would go to bed and sleep well into morning.

FIFTEEN

Clint tumbled into bed but not before making sure that the deadbolt on his door was locked and, for extra measure, a chair was wedged under the door handle. Before retiring, he had spent an hour visiting Bodie's other popular saloons but had neither seen Ian Palmer nor anyone that resembled the Vacca brothers. As for Jessie Lane, Clint had avoided the old highwayman's saloon, not wanting to become involved in a fight with Lane if it could be avoided.

Clint slept well past nine and was awakened by a loud knock at his door. Grabbing his six-gun and still half-asleep, he demanded, "Who is it?"

"Abe Timber. Open up."

It was the old liveryman. Clint tossed his bedsheets aside and shuffled to the door, the Colt still clenched in his hand because the liveryman could have a gun at his back. Jessie Lane or one of the Vacca brothers would have no compunction about forcing Abe to get an unsuspecting victim to open his door.

"Step back against the far wall," Clint ordered, pulling on his pants and moving to the left of the door. He unbolted the lock and pulled it open, careful not to expose his body to sudden fire.

"Damn, you're a cautious man, ain't you?" Timber said.

Clint surveyed the otherwise empty hallway. "Caution and being suspicious have kept me alive so far. Come on in."

"Can't stay but a minute. I'm takin' a mighty big risk just comin' here."

"Why?"

"There's some fellas by the name of Vacca. I hear tell that they're hunting for you."

"So why are you risking your life to warn me?"

"Because I remembered who you are—the Gunsmith. I heard stories about you and figured you deserved a fighting chance."

Clint went over and began to dress. "I wonder how they heard of me being in town."

"The word got around about that big pile of money you won from Mr. Meeks last night. He's the town character and you exposed him for bein' a cheat. Word travels fast and Mr. Meeks also let it be known that you were lookin' for this Ian Palmer fella."

Clint shook his head. "It sounds like everyone in Bodie knows the reason for my being here."

"Yep." The old liveryman squinted his eyes and then he pulled out a piece of paper and extended it to Clint.

"What's this?"

"It just says that, if you get yourself killed, I get that fine black gelding, your saddle, bridle and your six-shooter."

"What?"

"Well, I'm the only one that had the guts to warn you, ain't I? I figure that means I deserve something."

Clint glanced down at the note. It was full of misspellings and crudely written, but it would probably hold up

THE DEADLY DERRINGER 119

in Bodie. What the hell, he thought, I do owe this old conniver something.

"All right." He scribbled his name and handed the paper back to Timber. "I suppose this means that you're hoping I get planted in your cemetery."

Abe Timber scratched himself vigorously before he answered. "I don't wish you to die, but I could make a tidy profit off your horse and belongings. Why, that gun of yours alone is probably a museum piece. I figure it might bring as much as a thousand dollars."

Clint summoned up a thin smile. "Is Jessie Lane also out gunning for me?"

"I don't know, but I doubt it. He ain't as old and as stove in as me, but he's too old to be a gunfighter anymore. My guess is that he's just sitting back with a big smile on his face as he waits for them Vacca brothers to take target practice on your hide."

Clint supposed this made sense. Jessie was smart and he wasn't the kind of man to take unnecessary chances.

"But nobody has heard of a man named Ian Palmer?"

"I didn't say that."

Clint finished strapping his six-gun around his waist. "I haven't the time for guessing games. What have your heard about Palmer?"

"I heard there's a man who calls himself Wade Parker who fits the description for the one you're hunting. He's a gambler that hangs out in the Nevada Saloon."

"I must have missed it last night. Where is it?"

"Clear at the far end of town."

Clint was completely awake now. "Do you know where he might sleep?"

"I heard he's got a woman on Virgin Alley. That's where all Bodie's ladies of the night live."

"And her name?"

Timber stepped back into the hallway. "Give me twenty dollars and five minutes and I can find out. I hear that you won a couple hundred dollars from Mr. Meeks last night."

"He was dealing from the bottom of the deck," Clint said. "Even so, I let him walk away unharmed."

"Then twenty dollars shouldn't trouble you at all," Timber said with a toothless grin.

"All right. Go find out where this Wade Parker fella is right now."

"I'll do it, but I want ten dollars now and ten when I come back." Timber winked. "I can't take the chance that them mean Vacca boys might kill you before I get back."

Clint had to restrain himself from reaching out and grabbing the old hustler by his throat and straightening him up permanently. Fists knotted with anger, he went and got ten dollars from his jacket, then paid Timber.

"Five minutes," he said. "If you aren't back by then, I'm leaving."

"I'll be back," Timber promised before he scuttled down the dim hallway and disappeared with more speed than Clint would have thought possible of one so bent.

Amazingly, Timber was back in less than three minutes. He was out of breath and looked very excited. "All hell is going to break loose!"

"What do you mean?"

"The Vacca brothers are coming. Hell, they're right on my heels!"

Clint grabbed Timber's six-gun and his own saddlebags with extra cartridges. "I'm going to need to borrow your gun. Where is this Parker fella?"

"But you ain't got time to find him!"

"Where is he?"

"He sleeps with a woman named Sweet Sally."

"And where can I find her—exactly?"

Timber quickly gave Clint a rush of directions and then Clint was flying out the door, racing down the hallway to the last room, which he hoped faced into the alley.

Clint tried the door. He could hear shouting in the lobby and he was pretty sure that it would be the Vacca brothers. The door in front of him was locked. Clint could hear a man's and a woman's voices. He reared back and kicked the door in.

The man was on the woman and they were locked together but Clint didn't take more than a glance as he shot across the room, grabbed the window and yanked it open. He peered down. It was a fifteen-foot drop to the alley, more than Clint wanted, but there was no choice. Trapped upstairs, outnumbered five to one, he had no chance at all against five hard and determined men.

"What the hell?" the man cried, still unwilling to relinquish his dominant position on the woman.

"Sorry," Clint said, removing his Stetson, then tossing it and his saddlebags filled with his belongings and last night's winnings through the window. He shoved a leg outside and looked back once more at the pair in bed.

They were both at least fifty pounds overweight and the bedcovers had fallen from their heaving bodies. Clint found the sight of their sweaty coupling offensive but knew that he owed them the courtesy of a warning. "Folks," he said, "I think you're going to have a whole lot more company in about one minute."

"Dammit, what's going on here?"

Clint didn't think there was time to explain so he pushed out the window, dangled for a moment and then dropped with a grunt to the alley. Before he could scramble to his feet and replace his hat on his head, the man shoved his bare shoulders out the window.

"Sorry," Clint said again.

The man started to answer but a hand clamped on his shoulder and he was jerked back inside. He disappeared and a hatchet-faced Vacca with black eyes and heavy brows shoved a gun out the window.

Clint's own hand streaked for his six-gun and it came up. Even though Vacca fired first, his shot was wide. Clint did not miss. His bullet struck the gunman just under his jaw and ripped up through his brain to explode out the back of his skull.

Clint turned and ran. He was going to visit Virgin Alley. With any luck at all, he'd find this so-called Wade Parker asleep beside Sweet Sally and end this affair right sudden.

Abe Timber's instructions had been hurried but accurate. Clint skidded to a halt at the east end of Virgin Alley and remembered that the old man had said that Parker's woman lived about halfway down this row of cribs on the right.

It was still much too early for the ladies to be up and about, so Clint was at least spared the distraction of having a bunch of aggressive women trying to hustle him.

He ran down the alley with its colorful little cribs, many decorated with planted flowers. In front of most of the cribs were baskets of women's underthings which an ancient Chinese laundryman was collecting to be washed and returned before another night of business.

Clint had seen many Virgin Alleys in his time. Almost every Western town of any size had one and they were all very much the same. At night, red, green or yellow lanterns were often placed by the entrances of each girl's crib and they would stand under them, half-dressed and in some provocative pose.

Some of the girls were pretty but that didn't last long. A year or two of this mean existence and even the loveliest of them became hard and calculating. The cape of darkness hid much of the ugliness of these places, but in the early morning light, the squalor and desperateness of the situation was sobering.

Abe Timber had told Clint to look for a crib with a purple lightshade and when Clint found it, he paused, drew his six-gun and went to the door. He knew that the Vacca brothers would be coming up his back trail, more determined than ever because of the death of one of their number and that there was no time for politeness.

Clint opened the door of the crib and peered into the darkness. The single, grubby room reeked of smoke, whiskey and other odors that Clint did not even want to consider.

"Miss Sweet Sally?" he asked, peering into the darkness.

In answer, Clint saw a movement and something told him to jump aside. It was well that he did because a bullet occupied his vacated space. Another shot followed and Clint heard a curse and then the sound of wood splintering.

Parker was bursting out the back of the crib! Knowing he'd be shot if he went back inside, Clint turned with every intention of going around to the back of the cribs.

"There he is!" someone shouted.

Clint twisted around just in time to see four tall, very determined Vacca brothers skid around a corner and fill the entrance to Virgin Alley. The Gunsmith did not wait to feel his body become riddled by bullets. Even though he was sure that Sweet Sally would kill him when he jumped inside her crib, there seemed no choice but to pay her a visit.

Ducking his head and with his gun in his fist, Clint threw himself into the crib. He struck Sweet Sally in the darkness and the sound of her gun filled his ears. Clint felt a bullet crease his shoulder. He tripped over something and plowed headlong into a nightstand. A stinking chamber pot crashed to the floor and the smell of it burned Clint's nostrils.

Sweet Sally screamed as if she was being attacked. Half-dressed, she tromped on Clint with both feet and lunged outside.

"He's in here! The Gunsmith is in here!"

Half-blind, Clint tore a piece of clothing that had entangled his boots. He wasted precious moments fumbling around for his saddlebags. There was no time to search in the darkness for his Stetson so he jumped back to his feet and, knowing he'd die if he went out the front door of the crib, he bulled his way through the broken back wall of Sweet Sally's crib.

Parker or Palmer or whoever it was had vanished. Clint had no idea where to run but he knew that run he must. He spotted a horse tied to the back of a crib about a hundred yards up the alley. If he could reach that animal and get into the saddle before the Vacca brothers burst into view, he might have a chance of escaping with his life and fighting on his own terms instead of theirs.

Clint sprinted for the horse. He was still forty feet from it, however, when bullets began to whine like hornets all around him. Knowing he'd never reach the horse, much less mount it before being killed, Clint threw himself sideways between another set of cribs.

He was getting out of Bodie, but he'd come back later.

SIXTEEN

Clint was not leaving without Duke. On his own tall, swift horse, the Gunsmith felt confident he could outrun any of the pursuing Vacca brothers. But on someone else's horse, Clint realized full well that he might be run down somewhere out in the Nevada high-desert country and killed.

With that thought foremost in his mind, Clint made his way back to Abe Timber's livery with a gun in one fist and a spare tucked under his waistband. He knew that time was not on his side and it rankled him badly to have to leave Bodie on the run. But sometimes, the man who ran lived to fight another battle and Clint figured he had a few more battles left in him to win.

Reaching the back door of Abe Timber's livery, Clint paused to catch his breath for a moment, then he stepped inside and moved quickly to Duke's stall. His saddle was just where he'd left it the night before and Duke nickered a familiar welcome.

"I'm afraid we've got to make a fast exit from Bodie," he told the gelding as he holstered his six-gun and grabbed his bridle. "But we'll be back soon."

The light was poor inside the cavernous livery, but Clint could see that Duke had been curried and when he bitted the gelding and led him out to be saddled, he was also pleased that Abe had shod the animal.

Clint reached over and placed his saddle blanket on Duke's back, then grabbed his saddle and heaved it up in place. He was just reaching under the horse for his cinch when a voice said, "Freeze."

Clint froze because the voice was accompanied by the cocking of a gun.

"Put your hands up and turn around real slow."

Clint knew who it was before he even turned. "So," he drawled, "I hear you're too old to be a highwayman so now you're robbing drunken miners at your card tables, huh, Jessie?"

"You sonofabitch," the man hissed as he came full face with Clint. "I've dreamed of a moment like this for years."

Clint studied the man. Jessie Lane had once been a big, barrel-chested brawler. Now, he appeared to have shrunk. He wasn't tall anymore and his once-broad shoulders now drooped; his face was mottled and looked unhealthy.

"Time hasn't been very good to you, has it, Jessie? You're a sick old man."

The gun shook in Jessie's big, liver-spotted fist. "I may be old, but this gun in my hand says I'll outlive you!"

"Maybe." Clint lowered his hands just a little. "I will say this, your brains are still working or else you wouldn't have figured out where I'd head on the run."

"I knew you couldn't leave without Duke," Jessie said, his voice boastful. "I remembered how much stock you put in that animal and how it was the only thing that allowed you to overtake me that time down in Texas."

"Congratulations."

"I always wanted that gelding for myself."

THE DEADLY DERRINGER

"Too bad, because you're way too old to ride him now," Clint said with a sad shake of his head. "Truth is, Jessie, this big gelding would buck you off."

Jessie's lips pulled back from his teeth. "I will say this, Gunsmith, you never lacked for grit. And you always had more luck than anyone I ever knew."

"You call it luck, I think it has something to do with being smart and knowing how vermin like you will act when cornered."

Jessie's gloating smile turned sour. "You bastard. The only reason I haven't shot you already is that the Vacca brothers will torture you. They've talked about it for as long as we've known each other."

"Doesn't surprise me," Clint said, deciding that it would be vastly preferable to have this man kill him than to be handed over to the Vacca men. "You're all cut from the same vicious mold."

The pistol began to shake again in Jessie's fist and Clint inwardly steeled himself for a bullet. He was just about to throw himself sideways and make a rolling dive for his six-gun when Abe Timber burst through the back doorway.

"Clint, I . . ."

Jessie turned and in that one unguarded split second, Clint's hand streaked downward for the Colt on his hip. The gun jumped into his hand and swept upward in a single, incredibly smooth motion.

Too late did Jessie Lane realize his mistake. Caught half-turned, he made a desperate attempt to turn back and shoot the Gunsmith but a bullet slammed him over backward. He hit the dirt, skidded, and then cursed with his dying breath.

"Get out of here!" Clint shouted to the confused liveryman. "You don't want any part of this!"

"Goddamn right I don't!" Timber shouted, reversing directions and shooting back outside.

Clint grabbed his saddlehorn and despite his wounds, he had no trouble swinging into his saddle. He ducked his head as Duke shot out the door and when he saw the Vacca brothers coming on the run, he emptied his gun to scatter them and give himself a few additional precious seconds before Duke carried him down a side street, then out of town.

The Gunsmith slowed Duke to a trot just a mile out of Bodie. If the Vacca brothers were coming after him, he wanted to see them on his back trail and start thinking about laying a trap.

Ten minutes later, Clint spotted the four galloping horsemen and a cold grin shaped his mouth.

"They must want me real bad and I can't say that I find it surprising. After all, counting the one I shot today, that makes three whose one-way tickets to hell I've punched."

Clint waited until his pursuers were less than two miles behind him and then he touched Duke with the rowels of his spurs. He really did not know this surrounding high-desert country very well, which was to his disadvantage. However, he had the best horse and the added advantage of knowing that they wanted to kill him so bad they would be reckless.

Duke settled into an easy lope that he could sustain across many miles. "We'll just find ourselves some narrow canyon," Clint said, constantly looking over his shoulder and judging the distance, "and then we'll spring a big surprise on those boys."

In answer, the tall, black gelding flicked its ears and kept its head down and minded its own earnest business.

By noon, Clint could see that the Vacca brothers had stopped attempting to overtake him. They had made several hard rushes to close the distance and it had taken a lot out of their horses without any gains. The distance between them and the Gunsmith had not varied more than half a mile all morning.

Clint had led them to the west, toward the distant Sierras, whose highest peaks were still capped with mantles of snow. He might just as well have ridden in any other direction but his thinking was that the mountains would offer more opportunities for ambushing the determined brothers. There would be forests, canyons and lakes. He might even be able to cover his tracks in a mountain stream and double back on the Vacca men to catch them from behind.

And there was one other factor. He'd been in such a hurry to leave his hotel room after being warned by Abe Timber that he had forgotten to grab his Winchester. So now he had two six-guns, but that would not do him much good out in open desert country. The Vacca men would have Winchesters and they'd be able to pull him into their firing range. The moment they accomplished this, Clint had no doubt their first order of business would be to drop his horse. Once Clint was afoot in the desert, the outcome of this deadly game would already have been decided.

When Clint reached the forested foothills, he slowed his horse to a jog and when he came upon a clear mountain stream, he allowed Duke to drink as much as he pleased. Clint even dismounted himself and drank his fill before climbing back into the saddle and pushing on up through the pines.

All afternoon, he rode steadily higher into the mountains, only occasionally catching a glimpse of the four riders glued to his back trail. Clint kept watching for a good ambush point but did not see one. The stream he'd followed had fed down into a wide canyon and the trail was marked with fresh hoofprints.

It was nearly sunset when he came upon a cabin nestled in a small meadow. Clint saw a handsome Appaloosa horse in a pine-pole corral and a large black dog came out to bark at his appearance. A moment later, the cabin door opened and a figure appeared carrying a hunting rifle.

The Gunsmith was a little upset with himself for bringing a load of trouble to the doorstep of this innocent mountain settler. He could have simply ridden around the cabin and continued up the canyon but that might well have sealed the homesteader's fate. The Vacca brothers, not wanting any witnesses and also in need of supplies, would take a fresh horse, a hunting rifle and whatever else they could carry after killing this man.

"Hello!" Clint yelled, his voice echoing up the canyon.

The figure at the doorstep did not wave the Gunsmith forward in greeting but stood immobile. It was a rather smallish man dressed in a heavy wool coat, baggy pants and a black slouch hat.

Glancing over his shoulder and not seeing the Vaccas but knowing they would have heard his call, Clint knew he had little choice but to approach the cabin and explain the circumstances. Then, the man with the rifle had two choices, he could run or he could join Clint and fight.

"I could use some help," Clint said, taking care to keep his hands out from the gun on his hip. "I'm in a little trouble."

"I got troubles enough of my own," the settler called, "so ride on by!"

"I can't," the Gunsmith said when he was less than fifty yards from the rifle-toting settler. "There are four

THE DEADLY DERRINGER 131

killers behind me. If I ride on, they'll most likely kill you for that fine rifle and Appaloosa horse."

"They can try," the settler said with his rifle trained on Clint's chest.

Clint squinted, looking closer. He sighed with dismay to realize that this settler was just a boy of about fourteen.

"That's far enough," the boy said, putting the big Sharps rifle to his shoulder and taking aim.

Clint jerked Duke to a quick standstill. "Kid, I'm sorry to bring you trouble but I can't leave you here alone. Those men following me are without conscience or mercy."

The boy didn't look convinced and his huge black dog was anything but friendly. It was snarling and its hackles stood raised on end.

"Easy, Bear," the boy said, glancing at the dog, then turning to Clint and saying, "Ride on, mister. I don't know what you're doing up this canyon, but just ride on and no one will get hurt."

"That's not true," Clint said. "If it was, I'd do as you say."

"You'll do it anyway," the boy said, taking dead aim. "And you'll do it before I count to three. One."

"Listen to me!"

"Two."

Clint wasn't waiting to have that big rifle drill a hole like a small plate through his chest so he spurred Duke hard and the animal jumped forward. Clint reined it up-canyon and was about fifty yards away when he heard a rifle shot.

He twisted around in his saddle just in time to see the boy dodge a bullet and sprint for his cabin with Bear on his heels.

The Vacca brothers broke from the trees and came charging across the meadow.

"Aw, hell," Clint swore as he reined Duke around and drew Timber's six-gun from his belt. He opened fire and just as he came even with the cabin, the Sharps boomed like a small cannon and one of the Vacca men was jerked from his saddle as if by an invisible wire.

Clint reined Duke in hard behind the cabin as the Sharps boomed a second time. He dismounted and when he reached the corner of the cabin, he saw that the three remaining Vacca brothers were in full retreat. They reached the safety of the trees and vanished.

"Nice shooting!" Clint yelled. "I'm back."

In answer, the Sharps blasted a hole through the mud plastering packed between the cabin walls. Had Clint been standing a foot to his right, the shot would have torn him in half.

"Hey! We got to stick together! Those three will be coming for us after dark."

There was no answer. Clint took a deep breath and considered what he was going to have to do next. It was clear that the boy was a marksman and trusted no one. Just earning the boy's confidence might be a fatal undertaking.

SEVENTEEN

A bullet screamed in at Clint and he jumped back from the corner of the cabin with a two-inch long splinter sticking out of his forearm. He yanked the splinter free, gritting his teeth.

"Hey, kid!" he shouted. "They're going to circle this cabin and come in at us from three sides. We'd do a whole lot better if we fought them together."

"It's *your* fight, mister! I don't want nothing to do with them men."

Clint had to curb his mounting impatience. "Listen kid, you *killed* one of them out in that meadow. You think they're going to be satisfied with just getting even with me, now?"

There was no answer. Several more bullets came slamming in to strike the cabin near Clint. He knew that the Vacca brothers were on the move, hoping to get around to where they could get a clear shot at him.

"Make up your mind, kid! We either get together or I have to get out of here. What's it going to be?"

"Who are you?"

"Does it matter?" Clint shouted with exasperation.

"Yeah."

"My name is Clint Adams. I'm also called the Gunsmith. The men trying to kill us are the Vacca brothers and they want me because I killed their other brothers."

"Why?"

" 'Cause they were no damned good!"

There was a moment's silence and just when Clint was ready to give up and make a dash for some cover, the kid said, "All right. I got Bear tied, come on inside. I'm swinging the door open now."

Clint didn't have to waste any time thinking about moving for cover. He made a wild dash around the corner of the cabin with bullets flying around him and he covered the last ten feet to safety in a long, low dive through the cabin door.

The boy slammed the door shut as a swarm of bullets hammered into wood. Bear, hackles up and a deep rumble in his chest, lunged against a heavy chain; his snapping fangs ended up less than a foot from Clint's throat. The interior of the cabin was too dim to see well, but Clint could smell Bear's foul, hot breath.

Clint crabbed back from the beast. "Tell him I'm on *your* side," he said, more worried about the huge, ferocious dog than any of the Vacca brothers.

The boy grabbed his lunging, snarling dog by the tail and dragged the beast away. "No, Bear! No, Bear!"

Slightly unnerved by the huge dog's very near miss at tearing open his throat, Clint shook his head and scooted around toward the door. He pushed it open a little and this brought more bullets from the surrounding forest.

Clint was about to speak when he heard the sound of coughing in the darkness and realized that there was someone else in the cabin.

"Who's that?"

"It's my father," the boy said. "He's real sick."

Clint pushed the cabin door shut and, careful to make

THE DEADLY DERRINGER 135

a wide circle around the still-snarling dog, he went to the rear of the cabin. As his eyes adjusted, he could see that the boy's father was lying on a bunk and was covered with a thin blanket.

"What's wrong with him?"

"Broke his leg going after a wounded buck. It's all turning black."

"Give me some light," Clint ordered.

The boy lit a candle and held it aloft over his father. The man's cheeks were sunken. He looked half-starved and there were dark circles around his eyes. It was easy to see that he was trying to act like a man but was on the verge of breaking down from the strain of taking care of his father.

Clint placed his hand on the man's forehead and it was hot to the touch. The man opened his eyes. "Who are you?" he whispered.

"I was just passing through. I'm afraid I brought you and your boy more trouble. There are men outside who want to kill me. I'd go away but I think they'd kill you and your boy anyway."

The feverish man blinked and said nothing. Clint did not know if he understood or not.

"Let's take a look at his leg," Clint said, slowly pulling back the blanket but already knowing that the man had gangrene from the putrid smell he now identified.

The leg had been broken halfway between the knee and the ankle. A jagged splinter of bone poked through flesh and the leg itself was at least twice its normal size. Long, black tentacles of poison reached up like fingers of death toward the man's torso.

"How long has it been since the accident?"

"About five days."

Clint shook his head. "He should have been brought down to a doctor the first day."

"I wanted to bring him down but he wouldn't hear of it. Said he'd be all right if he stayed to bed. Said a doctor would want to cut the leg off and even then he'd charge him too much money."

Clint turned away and hurried back to the door. "The leg is poisoning the rest of his body. It might already be too late because the poison might kill him even if the leg is cut off."

Clint started to say more but the sound of gunfire drowned out his words. When there was a momentary lull, he said, "Kid, I think your father is a dead man. I'm sorry."

The boy had been standing over his father but now he twisted around at Clint's words and yelled, "You don't know that! You're no doctor!"

Clint opened his mouth, then shut it before he said, "Yeah, you're right, kid. I'm no doctor. And I'm a man that's brought you even more troubles than you could already handle."

Clint reached out and pulled the door open. Bullets came flying inside the cabin and one hit something glass and shattered it in the darkness.

"What'd you do that for?"

Clint didn't answer right away. He peeked outside and saw what he needed to know. There was only one rifleman out in the trees directly in front. The other Vacca brothers would be moving into positions somewhere off to the sides or back of the cabin.

"What's the roof made of?" he asked.

"I don't know! Why, do you think they'll try to burn it?"

"Burn or drop down through it if they have to," Clint said.

The kid looked up at the roof. "Ain't but more logs."

THE DEADLY DERRINGER

Clint frowned. "I've chased outlaws a good many years and there's been a few times I was on the outside instead of the inside like now. If it was me out there, I'd get on the roof and find a niche where I could poke my rifle barrel into. Lever it just a little and the logs will pull apart. After that, it's just like shooting fish in a barrel. Or you can drop burning pinecones or needles down inside. It'll smoke up the cabin so bad no one can breathe."

"And then you shoot them down when they come out," the boy said.

"I always tried to give them a chance to surrender. Usually, they were coughing so bad they couldn't see to shoot straight."

The boy's expression was bleak. "So what do we do? I can't leave my father here."

Clint had already figured that much out. "If I thought that dog of yours could be trusted, I'd take him out there and let him help me even up the odds."

The boy was silent for so long that Clint wasn't sure that he'd understood. "Boy, did you hear me?"

"Yeah."

"Well, can I trust him to go after them and not me?"

"I don't know," the boy admitted. "Bear isn't one to trust anybody."

"He'd make a big difference," Clint said. "If he could go after that rifleman out front, I could reach cover and try to kill the two we can't see yet."

The kid nodded but it was plain that he didn't trust Bear not to attack Clint. The Gunsmith eased over to the kid's father. "Maybe if I wore something of his, it would carry his scent and that would make a difference."

"He's got an extra shirt."

Clint pulled off his own shirt. "Let me have it," he said.

A minute later, Clint finished buttoning up the sick man's shirt. He moved closer to the dog but said to the kid, "Tell him again I'm a friend."

The boy went to the dog. "Bear, friend," he said, taking Clint's own shirt and rubbing it across the dog who continued to growl menacingly.

"He sure isn't very friendly, is he?" Clint said.

"He's a good watchdog," the kid said. "That's why we took him."

"I've got to go," Clint said. "When I rush outside, I'll be going for the nearest cover I can find."

"That'd be the woodpile to the right."

"Okay. The man out front will open fire on me. You sic that dog of yours on him the minute I yell. Understand?"

"I sure wish you hadn't of come here."

"I know. I'm sorry about it myself but there's no use in worrying over that now. What's done is done. Ready?"

The boy nodded.

"Here we go," Clint said, gathering himself for a minute, then firing out the door on the run.

The rifleman got off two shots before Clint reached the woodpile and cover. He halfway expected one of the other brothers to shoot him from behind but when no shots were forthcoming, he knew that he now had a fighting chance.

"Okay!" he shouted at the cabin. "Let Bear loose!"

Seconds later, the huge black dog came flying out the cabin door running low and hard. Clint saw the rifleman who'd fired on him suddenly move from cover and throw the gun to his shoulder as Bear closed the distance between the cabin and the forest.

The rifleman got off two shots but they were both far too hurried, and then Clint saw Bear leave the ground

THE DEADLY DERRINGER 139

and go for the Vacca brother's throat. The man screamed and went over backward to disappear in the trees. Clint crouched low, not even wanting to think about what was happening to the rifleman.

"Hector!" a man yelled. "Hector!"

Clint spun around to see one of the brothers come charging through the trees bent on helping his poor brother.

"Hold it!" the Gunsmith shouted.

The man twisted around and the rifle in his hands spat fire and lead. Clint felt the bullet narrowly miss his cheek as the gun in his own hand bucked twice and the running man crashed headfirst into a tree.

Clint ran to the dead man's side and grabbed his rifle, then dashed back to the woodpile where he crouched and waited.

"One to go," he said, trying to drown out the cries of the man being torn to shreds by Bear.

Clint did not have long to wait. He heard the sound of a man running through heavy brush and realized that the last brother was making a desperate attempt to reach and kill the dog that was on his brother.

The Gunsmith came to his feet and sprinted directly across the clearing and when he reached the man and the dog, he saw that it was already too late to save Bear's victim. The dog swung around on him and gathered itself to attack.

"No!" Clint shouted. "I'm a friend."

Bear seemed to hesitate a moment with indecision and that moment cost him his life as the last surviving Vacca brother shot the beast through the head.

Clint spun and fired three times before the man could lever another shell into his rifle. When the smoke cleared, he was the only thing left alive in the forest.

The Gunsmith turned and trudged back toward the cabin. The boy was crouched beside his father, rifle aimed at the open doorway.

"Kid, it's me," Clint said. "They're all dead."

A long silence. " And what about my dog?"

"He's dead too. He was a real fighter. Bravest dog I ever saw."

The boy's voice choked. "He hated strangers. We could never take him to a town. He'd have killed someone for sure."

Clint propped his Winchester up against the cabin wall. "What do you want to do about your father?"

"Would cutting off his leg save his life?"

"I don't think so," Clint said after long reflection. "I think he's already a goner."

"But you could at least try."

"Yeah," Clint said. "I owe you that much. I'll try if he wants. But ask him. It's his leg and his life. Most men know when they're dying and they don't want to be fussed with."

Clint stepped back outside the cabin. He went to find the Vacca brothers' horses. He also hoped that there was a decent shovel somewhere about because there were four bad men and a dog to bury. No, correction. The kid's father was going to die, too. The gangrene had spread too far.

"Five men and a dog," Clint muttered as he took a deep breath, thankful that he was still alive.

EIGHTEEN

The boy came out just as Clint was burying the last of the Vacca brothers in shallow, unmarked graves.

"I'd like to be the one that buries my dog," the boy said. "Pa wants to speak with you."

Clint nodded and handed the old shovel he'd found to the boy. "What's your name?"

"Josh Handley."

"Well, Josh," Clint said, "I'm real sorry about your Pa and your dog."

"You better hurry," Josh said. "I don't think my Pa has much time left."

Clint headed for the cabin with more than a little dread. He knew that the boy's father would have a few dying wishes concerning his son. Sometimes, Clint thought, a man can get rid of one set of troubles only to find himself saddled with others.

When he reached the man's bedside and pulled up a chair, the man with gangrene poisoning was so pale and still that Clint at first thought he might already be dead. But then Handley turned his head toward Clint and coughed.

"Just take it easy," Clint said. "You want some water?"

"No," Hadley whispered. "Josh says you're the Gunsmith. I heard about you."

Clint said nothing but instead leaned closer to listen.

"I want you to take Josh out of here and find him a home to live in. He's a good boy but he needs some schoolin'. A man can't trap or pan a livin' in these mountains no more."

"Is that what you've been doing here?"

"Yeah." Hadley reached out and gripped Clint's hand. "Will you swear to be honorable with Josh?"

"I do so swear."

"Then I can tell you there's a coffee can of gold nuggets buried under the floor. Josh knows of it. You make sure he don't get cheated out of it by townfolks."

"I'll take care of it," Clint vowed. "Your boy shot one of those men trying to kill me. That makes me beholden to him."

Josh's father closed his eyes. "I heard you were a good man. Reckon I heard right. I lost Josh's mother ten years ago. Now, I'm losing him. If I was goin' to live, it would be too damn hard anyway. I told Josh that but I ain't sure he understood."

Clint felt his throat squeeze. And even though the man did not make good sense, the Gunsmith understood his reasoning. "I'll see that your boy gets schooling and a good home. He's going to make a father proud."

The man's chin dipped either in understanding or appreciation, Clint guessed it didn't matter which. Knowing that Josh wanted to bury his dog himself, Clint went to catch Duke and the other horses. When he had all the animals penned in the Hadley corral, Clint walked slowly back across the meadow. The dog was buried and Josh had gone back inside the cabin.

It was an hour before sunset when Josh came out again and Clint needed just a glance at the tears rolling down

THE DEADLY DERRINGER   143

the boy's cheeks to realize that Hadley was dead.

"We ought to bury him right away," Clint said.

Josh nodded and they got the job done before sundown. Clint left Josh by his father's grave as he cooked up a batch of salt pork, beans and potatoes. When the boy finally came in way after dark, Clint said, "Food is on the stove, still hot."

"I ain't hungry."

"You've got to eat," Clint said. "You're already too thin."

"I just can't."

Clint would not take no for an answer. "Listen," he said gently, "your father asked me to take care of you. Find you a good home. He wanted you to get some schooling and to make him proud. You can't do that if you starve."

Josh thought about that for several minutes before he took the plate and forced himself to eat.

The next morning, Josh and Clint found the coffee can full of gold nuggets.

"That's more of a stake than most men start out with in this world," the Gunsmith said. "If you use it smart, that much money will buy your future."

"What does that mean?"

"It means that you ought to put it in a good bank for safekeeping, get some education and then figure out how you want to invest the money. Maybe it will get you a start-up herd of cattle or a small ranch."

"I don't want to ranch."

"Then a store or . . ."

"I'd like to be a mustanger. I favor horses over most anything," Josh said.

"I understand that," Clint told him. "But even mustanging takes money. You need it to buy horses, saddles, ropes and provisions."

Josh didn't say anything but Clint knew the boy's mind was working and that he was smart enough to know Clint was telling him the truth.

When their horses were saddled, the Gunsmith tied the four Vacca brothers' horses head to tail and led the way back down the canyon.

"Where are we headed?" Josh asked when they stopped to rest at noon on the edge of the forest with a vast sea of Nevada sagebrush stretching out before them.

Clint frowned. "I need to make a decision right about now. I'm searching for a gambler named Ian Palmer. He's killed a lot of good men, Josh, and he'll kill more if I don't stop him."

"Then we'll go find him," Josh said as if it were a simple matter.

But Clint shook his head. "The thing of it is, I need to get you to some friends and then go hunt Palmer by myself. A man never knows when he'll die and I don't want to leave your father's dying wish unfulfilled."

"I figure I'm old enough to look out for myself," Josh said, his eyes flashing with defiance. "I don't need your help—or anyone else's."

Clint was sitting on a rock and he turned to regard the boy thoughtfully. He remembered how, when he was Josh's age, his pride had usually clouded his good sense. A fourteen-year-old boy wanted to think of himself as a man. Josh had even killed one of the Vacca brothers with that big Sharps rifle now resting in his saddleboot, but killing or not, he still wasn't a man.

Clint frowned and studied the desert country they were about to enter. The thing of it was, he could not come right out and tell Josh that a killing didn't make him a man. It

THE DEADLY DERRINGER 145

would just make a proud boy who'd suddenly lost his father and his dog angry enough to ride off alone.

"Well, maybe I could use your help," Clint conceded.

Josh really looked at him. "You mean that?"

"I do. The man I'm hunting shot me in the head with a hideout derringer that springs into his hand from up his sleeve."

"I'll help find him."

"Might be that I could use someone I could trust to sort of watch my back."

For the next half-hour, Clint told Josh about Miss Joanna Rogers and how Palmer had treated her so bad and then shot her in the hip at Virginia City.

"She's a beautiful girl, but the doctor figures she'll never dance again or even walk without a limp."

"I'm glad that I'll be helping you find a man like that," Josh said. "It's the kind of a thing that would have made my Pa proud of me."

"He was already proud," Clint said, coming to his feet and tightening his cinch. "We've just got to find that rattlesnake and take care of unfinished business."

"You just going to gun him down?"

"No," Clint said. "I've always given a man a chance. Always. I can't change the way of it now. I'll give Ian Palmer or whatever he's calling himself a fair chance to surrender and go before a judge and jury. Of course, he knows he'll hang. That's why I'm sure he'll use that derringer again."

"But you'll be ready."

"Yeah," Clint said. "But from what I've heard and the fact that he got it out faster than I could shuck my own six-shooter, I don't know how ready any man could be against that kind of a rig."

"If he kills you this time," Josh said, patting the butt

of his Sharps rifle, "I'll make sure he doesn't live to earn anymore of a reputation."

Clint's lips tightened in silence. The last thing he wanted was to send Josh Hadley down the gunslinger's road.

"Let's mount up."

"Where are we going to start the search?"

"I guess that, if I were Palmer, I'd stay in Bodie."

"I heard of Bodie," Josh said. "I heard it was a hard place to make a living but an easy place to die."

"That's about the way of it," Clint said. "And if we trail these four Vacca brothers' horses into town, people will recognize them and all hell might break loose."

"Then maybe we'd better sell them and their saddles before we reach Bodie."

Clint nodded his head. He thought that was an excellent idea. "There's a stage stop just north of Bodie with some good men. I think maybe they'd be willing to buy these horses."

"Then let's go," the kid said. "And maybe before we get to Bodie you could show me the fast draw."

"The way of the gun is one I'm trying to shed," Clint said. That's why I gave up being a lawman and turned to gunsmithing for a living."

Josh Hadley shook his head. "Those dead men would never believe that."

"I only killed two. You shot one and your dog killed the other."

The boy didn't argue or say another word as they rode on toward Bodie.

NINETEEN

When Clint and Josh reached the desert stage stop just a few miles above Bodie, Ben Wilson, Dade Catlow and Charley Benson were reclining on the front porch of their little station sipping on a jug of whiskey.

"Well, if it isn't a ghost from the past!" Wilson said, dropping his heavy boots down to the earth and coming to his feet. "We thought sure that you were a a dead man when we heard that all four of the Vacca brothers lit out on your back trail."

Clint turned to the riderless horses that he led. "As you can see, they won't be riding anymore."

"Well, I'll be damned," Catlow whispered. "So you shot all four of them?"

"I had some help," Clint said. "Boys, this is Josh Hadley. He's been living in the mountains trapping and helping his father pan the streams for gold."

"Didn't know there was any placer gold left after the forty-niners and the Chinamen went over all them streams with a fine-toothed comb."

Josh spoke right up. "There's always fresh gold gets washed down from the mountaintops every spring with the runoff. It isn't going to make a man rich, but it kept us in vittles and ammunition."

"Well, I'll be damned," Benson said. "Maybe we ought to go up there next spring and shut this damned station down."

"I don't think you'd like it," Josh said with a hint of disapproval. "It's a lot harder than sitting in chairs all day, sippin' from a jug."

Wilson's cheeks colored with embarrassment but the other two men laughed out loud.

"Josh speaks his mind," Clint said.

"He sure as hell does," Wilson grunted. "Light down and have a pull on this jug."

"Don't mind if I do," Clint said, dismounting. He drank deeply and felt the fire burn down his parched gullet. "That's not bad liquor," he said in a husky voice.

"It's damned *good* liquor," Ben Wilson said. "So did those horses really belong to the Vacca brothers?"

"That's right." Clint pulled his Stetson down low over his eyes. "All four are dead and I saw no point in leaving their horses to roam. So we brought them down to sell."

"They'll get you in deep, deep trouble," Wilson warned. "As mean as they were, the Vacca brothers still had plenty of friends. Why, you wouldn't ride fifty feet through Bodie before someone would blow you and the boy clean out of your saddles."

"I was afraid that you'd tell me that." Clint looked the station tender right in the eye. "So why don't *you* buy them?"

"What?"

"I'll sell them and their saddles, bridles and blankets real cheap. You or your men could trail 'em north to Reno or Carson City. None of the horses are branded."

Wilson shoved the jug at Clint and went to examine the four horses. He said, "From what I heard of the Vaccas,

THE DEADLY DERRINGER 149

they're almost sure to have stolen them."

"That's right," Clint agreed. "But they're good horses and saddles. Better than most you'd buy for fifty dollars."

Wilson's eyes narrowed. "Like I explained a few minutes ago, these horses could get someone killed."

"Only in Bodie."

"How much?"

"Thirty each."

"With the saddles?"

"That's right."

"What about the guns and rifles you must have taken?"

"We're keeping them." Clint said because he'd already inspected the Vacca brothers' weapons and found them to be of high quality and in excellent working condition.

"I'll pay you twenty-five for each horse and saddle," Wilson said.

Clint looked at Josh. They'd already agreed to split the proceeds. "What do you think, boy?"

"Uh-uh," Josh said. "Let's take them up to Carson City and make some real money."

"All right," Clint said, handing the jug back to Wilson and reaching for his saddlehorn to mount and ride away.

"All right, thirty dollars!"

"Thirty—cash."

"Cash," Wilson said, heading for the station.

"Old Ben," Catlow drawled when his employer was out of earshot, "he sure likes to drive a bargain."

"He just did, whether he'll admit it or not," Clint said.

"He knows that. He'll send me and Charley off to Carson with these horses and double his money. 'Course, it will cost him a little extra bonus for our trouble."

"Of course," Clint said as Wilson came out to pay him.

When the money had changed hands and they'd shaken to consummate the deal, Wilson said, "I have to ask you something."

"Go ahead."

"Why didn't you and the boy take the horses up to Carson or Reno yourselves? It's not that far and it would have been worth your trouble."

"I know," Clint said, "but we're on our way to Bodie."

All three men gaped with astonishment.

"What the hell for?" Wilson asked. "That ought to be the last place you want to go."

"It's like I explained the last time I was on my way to Bodie," Clint said, "I mean to find Ian Palmer and either shoot him down or take him to a judge who will see that he hangs."

Catlow scratched his crotch and shook his head. "I sure would hate to see you take a boy like that along. I figure that you've about run your luck out as far as it will go and that the boy might also get caught in a crossfire."

"That's my choice," Josh said with real anger. "I handled myself against the Vacca brothers. I can help the Gunsmith about as well as the next man."

The three station men exchanged glances and perhaps wisely chose not to comment.

"We'll be riding as soon as we water our horses," Clint said.

"You're welcome to some good water, same as the last time."

"Much obliged," the Gunsmith said as he mounted Duke and glanced up at the sun. It occurred to him that he'd be arriving in Bodie just about the same time he had before—shortly after sunset. That was good.

THE DEADLY DERRINGER 151

• • •

When Clint and Josh arrived at the livery, old Abe Timber could not believe his eyes. "What the hell are *you* doing back here?"

"Unfinished business," Clint said. "I still haven't found Ian Palmer."

"You must be loco! What happened to the Vacca brothers? You give them the slip?"

"Not exactly. Abe, this is my friend, Josh Hadley. Josh is a pretty fair shot with that big Sharps in his saddle boot."

Abe glanced at Josh but then studied his Appaloosa much more carefully. "Hell of a nice horse," he said. "Interested in sellin' him?"

"Nope."

"With those markings, I'd be willing to give you fifty dollars."

"He's not for sale at any price," Josh said firmly enough to leave no doubt about changing his mind. "My father helped me break him. This horse is part of my father and I wouldn't sell him."

"Damned shame you feel that way," Timber groused.

The old man looked back at the Gunsmith who had dismounted and was already starting to pull his saddle off the sweaty back of his gelding.

"Whoa, up there!" Timber cried. "I can't let you keep these horses here!"

"Why not?" Clint demanded, slamming his saddle down on a saddle tree and then shaking out his blanket and turning it sweaty side up so that it would dry faster.

"Why, I already risked my neck for you once."

"Yes, and I paid you for it." Clint reached into his pants pocket. He knew full well that the old man was just angling for a payday. "How much this time?"

Timber's pale blue eyes shuttered. "What really happened to the Vacca brothers?"

"We killed them." Clint said simply. "They would have killed us if we hadn't. There was no other way."

Timber whistled softly. "Anyone see you ride in here?"

"No. We rode up the alley. Have you still got that piece of paper I signed giving you my horse and outfit if I'm killed?"

"I sure do."

"Give it back to me."

"Why?"

"Because it will eliminate the temptation to betray me," Clint said, extending his hand.

"Aw, come on!"

"Give it to me," Clint demanded.

Abe was actually carrying the paper and when he reluctantly gave it to the Gunsmith, Clint tore it to shreds. The old man looked devastated.

"Here," Clint said, handing him a roll of greenbacks. "There's at least fifty dollars in that roll. All I ask is that you take care of our horses and after they've been grained and curried, resaddle them and have them ready in case we need to get out of Bodie fast."

"You still going to try and find that same gambler fella?"

"That's right. You got anything new to tell me?"

"He came back to Sweet Sally for a couple of days. But I think he left her."

"Why?"

"Because she got drunk and raised so much hell two nights ago that they tied her up and sent her south in a freight wagon."

"Damn!" Clint swore. "Then where do I start looking?"

THE DEADLY DERRINGER 153

"Like I said," Timber drawled, "the man she was livin' with likes to deal cards at the Nevada Saloon. If he's still in town, that's where you'd find him."

"Wade Parker. Right?"

Timber nodded his head. "Wade Parker it is. What about the boy? A saloon of that type isn't any place for a kid."

"I'm no kid," Josh said hotly.

"Well, you ain't no full-grown man, either," Timber said with furrowed brows.

Timber was right about Josh not belonging in a saloon and Clint did not want the boy along if Parker and maybe some of his friends were waiting.

"I want you to stay here and help Abe with our horses. You'd just attract too much attention and I want to go into the Nevada Saloon without attracting *any* attention. You can understand that, can't you?"

"Yeah, but . . ."

"Listen," Clint said, "it's not that I don't think you're man enough to fight and die. It's just that I need to kind of slip into that saloon and find out if this Parker fella is the man I've been hunting. If he is, well, I'll just put a gun on him and hope everything goes peaceable. If he isn't, then we'll ride out tomorrow morning after we've eaten and had a good night's sleep."

"But what if this fella is sitting with a bunch of his friends?"

"Then maybe I'll come back for help," Clint said.

"You promise?"

"I promise."

"All right," Josh said. "But if you're not back in an hour, I'll come looking for you."

Clint nodded. If he wasn't back in an hour, he'd never be back—at least not in this life.

TWENTY

Clint checked his six-gun once more before he pulled his hat down low on his brow and slipped inside the Nevada Saloon. It wasn't much better or worse than most mining-camp saloons, though it did have a real bar instead of just some boards nailed across a keg.

No one paid the Gunsmith any attention because two powerful men were arm wrestling. The noise was deafening as spectators shouted wagers and the contestants grunted and even roared in their Herculean efforts.

Clint watched the crowd rather than the contestants. Not seeing anyone who even remotely resembled the gambler he sought, Clint shouted to the bartender, "I'll have a glass of beer."

The bartender quickly shoved a mug in the Gunsmith's hand. Clint reached for his money and said very offhandedly, "Do you see Wade Parker in here?"

"Hell," the bartender said. "He don't usually come in this early. Be in before long, though."

Clint paid for his beer, hooked his heel on the bar rail and leaned back to watch the contest with one eye and the batwing doors of the saloon with the other. But it wasn't easy. This was one of the best arm-wrestling matches he'd ever seen and the excitement was contagious.

One of the contestants was a squat, slope-shouldered man with a bald head heavily beaded with sweat. He wore a thick beard and his lips were drawn back from his big, yellow horse teeth. The sweaty Goliath had arms as big around as Clint's leg and he was straining until the tendons on his neck stood up like wires. He was winning too, but not by much.

His opponent was a sharp contrast. He was amazingly slender, though his shoulders were very broad. He was also quite tall and even with his face pale and his teeth gritted in effort, handsome. Clint had never been an arm wrestler, but watching these two men, it seemed to him that the taller man was able to make this a match only because he was extremely good at using his superior height and longer arm to gain leverage and afford himself a very crucial advantage. One thing was sure, his shorter opponent possessed far more brute strength.

Watching them, Clint thought it inevitable that the taller man would soon have his knuckles smashed against the table. Even as he was thinking this, however, the tall, handsome man growled and put on a tremendous burst of strength and, to the Gunsmith's utter amazement, staged a comeback. One shaky fraction of an inch at a time, the tall man brought his hand up until it was perpendicular.

The crowd screamed like wild men and even Clint found himself gripped by the titanic struggle.

"Ten dollars on the tall man," he yelled, yanking a bill from his pocket.

His bet was taken, but only after the hands stood at high noon and the tall man could not press his momentary advantage any farther.

"Another beer," Clint shouted, not taking his eyes off the contestants, whose eyes were beginning to bulge with strain.

"This could go on for hours," someone said. "It did the last time they went at it."

"Who won?"

"Ian Palmer," the bartender said very distinctly.

Clint almost dropped his beer. "Did you say Ian Palmer?"

"Yeah. He beat old Judd Raines but it took almost two hours."

Clint stared at the man he had sworn to kill or deliver to the gallows. Ian Palmer looked nothing like Clint had expected. He was much taller and far more powerful. His square jaw, dark, curly hair and glinting black eyes made him a striking figure and only now did Clint realize that Palmer was wearing a gambler's silk shirt whose sleeves were rolled up to his bulging biceps.

At least, Clint thought, he isn't going to spring the hideout derringer on me this time.

Clint finished his beer and smacked his lips. It would be insane to try to arrest Palmer before this match was decided. The other patrons would certainly tear him limb from limb if he interfered.

"There's Wade Parker," the bartender said, pointing to another handsome gambler who came striding through the door.

Clint shook his head. In truth, Wade Parker seemed exactly like the man Clint had been hunting. This gambler was also tall, but not as wide in the shoulders. And though good-looking in a raffish sort of way, there was about him an arrogance and a hardness that told Clint he was dangerous. Parker stood for a minute beside the door, then he grinned and walked around the contestants and took a chair at one of the poker tables and drew a deck of cards from his suit-coat pocket.

Clint turned his attention back to the arm-wrestling

contest. He no longer cared who won or lost, as long as the match ended soon and he had the drop on Ian Palmer.

And then, it suddenly ended. One minute the pair were straining, and then Ian Palmer thrust up to his full height, roared like a lion and bore the shorter man's hand down to the table. There was no smashing of knuckles, but it was a clear, clean victory and the crowd went wild with celebration.

Someone shoved his winnings into Clint's hand and he absently pushed the money into his pocket, then reached for his Colt, moving toward Ian Palmer, who was surrounded by a big crowd. Clint stood back and waited for an opening and then he drew his six-gun and fired a round into the ceiling.

Some men dived for the floor, others reached for their guns but Ian Palmer just stood facing Clint and the gun trained on his chest.

"What the hell is your problem?" Palmer demanded.

"I'm taking you up to Virginia City where you'll be charged with murder."

"What?"

"You heard me. You shot me and some poor drunk named Willard Myers down in Candelaria. Less than a week later, you shot a freighter to death near Dayton. You also shot Miss Joanna Rogers in Virginia City and . . ."

"Mister, you're insane!" the man cried. "I haven't been to Virginia City in three years and I've *never* been to Candelaria!"

"Tell that to the judge," Clint said. "Let's go!"

But the man shook his head. "I'm not going anywhere with you!"

"That's the Gunsmith!" someone shouted. "He gunned down one of the Vacca brothers along with Jessie Lane!"

Other men in the saloon shouted in agreement and

THE DEADLY DERRINGER 159

Clint retreated until his back was up against the wall.

The tall, powerful arm wrestler grinned coldly. "Mister, it looks to me like *you're* the one that's going to dance on the end of a rope instead of me."

"That may be," Clint said, "but Palmer, before I go down, I'll take you with me."

The man folded his arms across his chest. "My name isn't Palmer. Are you a crazy man?"

Clint blinked. "What do you mean, your name isn't Palmer?"

"It's Wade Parker. Has been for twenty-six years, ain't that right, boys? And the Vacca brothers have a lot of friends present in this saloon."

Clint tried to quell a rising sense of doom. He glanced at the bar but the bartender was gone. He swung his head around and the second gambler, the one with the hard eyes, was also gone.

Clint swallowed noisily. "I think maybe I've been hoodwinked," he said, trying to force a smile as he realized too late his mistake in assuming that the bartender would tell him the truth.

"You gonna put that gun away?" Wade Parker asked, advancing a step.

"I don't think so," Clint said, trying to slide along the wall toward the front door. "I think I'll just keep it in my hand until I get out of this saloon."

Clint was still inching toward the batwing doors when one of the patrons hurled a beer mug at him. He ducked and before he could straighten, two more mugs struck him, one full in the face and the other in the shoulder.

The Gunsmith went to his knees and the next thing he knew, it felt like a building was falling in on him. He was driven to the floor, beaten and kicked until darkness closed in and he no longer felt the pain.

TWENTY-ONE

Josh Hadley was about to run out of patience. Both his Appaloosa as well as Clint's black gelding had been fed, brushed and fussed over until there was nothing left to do but saddle the horses.

"I'm saddling them up now," Josh said to Abe Timber. "Clint said that I should in case we needed to get out of Bodie fast."

"Suit yourself," the old liveryman grunted. "But them horses need more than grain and curryin', they need a few days of rest."

"No time for that," Josh said, reaching for his saddle. He cinched it down tight, then said, "You got a hoof pick, Mr. Timber? Looks like my Appaloosa has picked up a rock."

Timber grumbled but he found a pick and gave it to the boy. Moving around so that he could watch Josh pry the rock out, he said, "That horse of yours wouldn't pick up rocks so easy if he was shod."

"Maybe not."

"You got any money? I could shoe him for . . . oh, five dollars."

"That's way too high," Josh said as he finished cleaning out the hoof, then set it down and went over to saddle

Clint's horse.

"Well, what's it worth to you then?"

"I might pay you a dollar."

"A dollar! Jeezus, boy! The shoes and nails alone cost a dollar in this town."

"All right," Josh said, "then two dollars."

"Four, and I'll give you some extra nails in case you lose a shoe."

"Three dollars," Josh said. "That's as high as I'll go."

Abe Timber wasn't pleased but since he had time on his hands, he nodded. "I'll fire up the forge."

Josh grabbed the Gunsmith's saddle blanket and placed it squarely on Duke's back. Next, he swung Clint's saddle across the gelding's withers, then cinched it down tight.

"Hey, Mr. Timber?"

"What?" Abe said, lighting his forge and using the old bellows to get the coal burning.

"It's been more than an hour since Clint left for that saloon, hasn't it?"

"I'd say it's been more like two hours."

Josh went to retrieve his Sharps rifle. He checked to make sure it was ready, then without a word of good-bye or explanation, he headed for the door.

"Hey, kid, just where do you think you're going?"

"I'm going to the Nevada Saloon to find the Gunsmith. He might be needing my help."

Timber wasn't pleased. "He said you should stay right here with me."

"Nope. He said to come along if he wasn't back in an hour," Josh countered. "And that's exactly what I aim to do. Which way to the Nevada Saloon?"

"Go right. It's about two blocks down. You can't miss it."

THE DEADLY DERRINGER 163

Josh checked his rifle. "I sure hope he's all right."

Timber scowled and released his bellows. "What if he ain't?"

"Then I'll do whatever I can."

"You might need some help," Timber grunted. "Wait a minute and I'll come along."

Josh waited. He was not familiar with towns and he knew that Bodie had a bad reputation.

"The Gunsmith took my six-shooter and never gave it back," Timber complained.

Josh went to a heavy canvas sack that was tied behind Clint's saddle. "Here," he said, pulling out several guns, "take your pick. They're all loaded."

Timber stared at them. "They belong to the Vacca brothers?"

"That's right. There was no sense in leaving good Colt revolvers in the forest to rust."

Timber selected a pair. "Better take a couple along, too," he said.

Josh took the old man's advice. He shoved two guns behind his waistband and followed Timber out the door, saying, "I sure hope there's no trouble."

Abe Timber didn't say a word as he hobbled along the boardwalk. They were less than a block from the Nevada Saloon when they saw the batwing doors swinging outward and Clint being dragged out by a mob.

"What are they going to do with him?" Josh cried.

"They're heading in the direction of the hanging tree at the north end of town," Timber said, coming to a dead stop. "Ain't nothing will save him now."

"We've got to try!"

But Timber shook his head. "And get ourselves riddled by bullets? No, thanks. I admire the Gunsmith and I'm sorry that he's ending up this way, but those boys mean business. You try to stop them and they'll likely hang you, too."

Josh gripped the Sharps until his knuckles were white. "I can't let him swing and I can't save him by myself. I need your help."

"I'm sorry," Abe said. "I enjoy life too much to throw it away on a man I hardly even know."

"I've got gold nuggets," Josh blurted. "A whole pocketful. I'd be willing to pay you."

Abe Timber folded his arms across his chest. "Boy, a dead man can't spend gold."

"But maybe you could just . . ."

"Just what?"

"Create a diversion of some kind!"

The old man's jaw dropped and his hands fell to his sides. "A diversion?"

"Sure, we could light a building on fire or something. That would give me time to reach Clint and set him free."

"What building?"

"How about your livery?"

"Hell, no!" Abe shook his head vigorously. "I ain't gettin' rich, but it puts food on the table."

Josh's mind was racing. "How much is it worth?"

"All of it?"

"Right now. Every board and stem of hay in the loft."

"Seven or eight hundred dollars, I reckon."

Josh shoved his hand into his pocket. "Here," he said, turning his hand over to reveal a fistful of gold nuggets. "These are worth that much and more. Take them!"

Timber stared at the nuggets. "Are you serious?" he whispered, taking the nuggets.

Instead of answering, Josh turned around and marched back to the livery. "Mr. Timber, why don't you get your horses out while I fire the loft. That ought to bring 'em running."

"Just like that?"

"There's no time for anything else," Josh said, snapping up the matches and lighting a kerosene lantern. "We're about out of time."

Josh took the lantern and climbed upstairs to the loft. He hurled the lantern into the dry hay and it ignited with a loud whoosh!

"Let's get out of here!" Josh cried, scrambling back down the ladder to help Abe lead their horses out the big front doors. Mounting his own Appaloosa, Josh ordered Timber to take Clint's horse out of harms way and hold it until he returned.

"You're crazier than he is!" Abe shouted.

But Josh didn't wait around to comment. He gave the Appaloosa its head and raced off toward Bodie's infamous hanging tree.

As he approached the crowd from the Nevada Saloon, he shouted, "Fire! Abe Timber's livery is on fire!"

The crowd's reaction was dramatic. Twice before fires had swept through Bodie and turned it to cinder and ash. Almost every able-bodied man in town belonged to a volunteer fire company and when they saw the flames licking from the second floor of Abe's livery, they forgot about the hanging and took off running for their fire companies.

Only the tall arm wrestler whom Clint had mistaken for Ian Palmer stood firm with a rope in his hand and the thick bough of a tree over his head. Josh rode up to him. "He goes free, mister."

"The hell he does! Get out of here, boy. The Vacca men were my friends."

"He goes free," Josh said, yanking his Sharps rifle from his saddle boot, "or you are going to die."

Wade Parker was fashioning a hangman's noose but at the sight of the big rifle, it slipped from his hand. He stared at Josh, measuring his determination.

"Who are you?"

"It doesn't matter, does it," Josh said.

"You light the fire?"

"I did."

"Maybe I'll see you get hanged too."

"I'll kill you if you don't walk away," Josh said, stepping down from his horse but never taking the rifle off his target.

Parker expelled a deep breath. "He your Pa?"

"My pa is dead," Josh said. "But he asked this man to look after me."

"Is that a fact?"

"Yes, sir. And he's a good man. We got to find Ian Palmer and kill him."

Parker glanced down at Clint, who was just beginning to stir. "Most likely, Palmer is long gone. Probably lit out for Lake Tahoe. He's got some friends on the south end of the lake. Maybe a woman, too."

"The Gunsmith won't stop until he finds him."

"He's in bad shape."

Josh took a step forward. "I know. But it isn't your problem."

Parker thought about that for several moments before he finally nodded. "Yeah," he said before he turned and walked away, "I guess that you're right."

As soon as the tall man was gone, Josh was at Clint's side. "Come on," he said. "We got to leave town in a hurry."

Clint shook his head and spat blood. "Uh, uh," he groaned. "I still have to find Ian Palmer."

"He's heading for Lake Tahoe."

THE DEADLY DERRINGER

"You sure?"

Josh considered the question for a minute, then he nodded his head. "Yes, sir, the tall man wouldn't have said so if it weren't true."

Clint nodded and let the kid help him to his feet. A moment later, Abe Timber arrived leading Duke.

The old liveryman dismounted and turned to stare up into the sky at the flames shooting out of his hayloft. Fire bells were clanging and the dark shadows of running men were everywhere.

"I hope Bodie burns right down to the ground," Abe said with vehemence in his voice. "It's a wicked town."

"Help me get the Gunsmith on his horse," Josh said.

Abe nodded and, together, they got Clint mounted.

"Did Parker do this to you?" Abe asked.

"He and about fifty others," Clint said. "I made a bad mistake."

"You can say that again," Abe grunted, climbing stiffly into his own saddle.

"Can you ride?" Josh asked.

Clint nodded. "I can get as far as the stage station and we can rest there until morning."

"Yes, sir."

Josh led the way out of Bodie. He didn't look back until he reached the rim of hills that surrounded the mining town. Then, twisting in his saddle, he surveyed the fire.

"They got your barn put out, Mr. Timber. Got the fire before it spread to the other parts of town."

"More is the pity," the old liveryman grunted. "And if I had my guess, I'd say that Bodie is just too wicked to die."

Josh turned away and led them north. He supposed that Abe Timber had things figured just about right.

TWENTY-TWO

Ian Palmer hadn't waited for the Gunsmith to discover that he'd been tricked by the Nevada Saloon bartender. Ian had just run for his horse and made tracks as if the devil himself were on his tail. He'd raced out of Bodie headed for Lake Tahoe and almost killed his mount before reaching that high mountain lake three days later.

But once back in the high mountains, Ian felt at home again. As a young man, he'd followed his father through the Sierra mining camps and found them to be comforting. Later on, when the gold had been panned out, he'd earned his living swamping saloons on the south shore of the lake. Catching the eye of a boozy old gambler named Dakota, Ian had been tutored very carefully on all the requisite skills necessary to be a frontier gambler.

"You need an edge," Dakota had always told him. "Every gambler needs an edge when Lady Luck is running away. I'll show you how to mark cards so that no one but another expert will know. I'll teach you how to shave a deck so fine that even a professional won't be able to tell for sure how you're cheating."

"What about dealing from the bottom?"

"I ain't going to show you that because it's what every man at the table is watching for when you start to win."

Over the years that had followed, Ian had learned his trade well. He'd prospered, in fact, and when he was twenty-one, he turned on Dakota one afternoon and said, "So long, old man."

Dakota's eyes were red from too much whiskey. His hands shook and he looked like a derelict. "I trained you, Ian. I need you now."

"Too bad."

"But I said I needed you! You *owe* me!"

"Here," Ian had said contemptuously as he'd tossed a silver dollar between Dakota's feet. "I owe you nothing more than a drink."

"Goddamn you! Come back here!"

But Ian had kept on walking and he'd never looked back at the pathetic old alcoholic. He'd just walked away hearing his curses. Two months later, in a rough logger's saloon at South Lake Tahoe, Dakota had been gunned down making a clumsy attempt to deal from the bottom of the deck.

Now, as Ian reined his horse in at that same lakefront saloon, he felt a quickening of his heart. Old Lars Andersen had been one of the first to log this country and when he'd been almost killed by a falling tree, he'd opened the Tahoe Saloon with the help of his wife, and daughter Helena. Helena with the golden hair and the enormous bust.

Ian had been the first man to make love to the big Swedish girl and she'd been madly in love with him for the next few years. He probably should have married her and saved himself a lot of trouble but he'd been too restless and in need of adventure. Maybe it was finally time to settle down. Maybe he would marry her at last and make all her fantasies come true. He'd take over her old man's prosperous saloon. Ian had always thought he could do a much better job.

"Ian? Is that you?"

Ian looked up from tying his horse and saw Joe Bean, a has-been logger who now operated a leaky little steamboat that ferried loggers back and forth across the lake in good weather.

"Yeah, it's me, all right."

Bean smiled. "It's been what, at least a year?"

"At least."

"You look like it's been a hard year," Bean said.

"Thanks, Joe. You look sort of run-down yourself. Is Helena working inside tonight?"

Bean nodded his head. He was a thin man with a long neck, sad eyes and a mouth that loved to gossip. "Sure, Ian, but she's with Bert Travis. They're engaged to be married."

Ian tried to hide his shock and alarm but he couldn't fool Bean. "Ha! I guess I know that you come looking for some lovin' and some of her daddy's money!"

"Shut up, you old fool," Ian said as he finished tying his horse and moving past the troublemaker.

"The weddin' is set for next week," Bean called after him as he stomped inside.

"We'll just see about that," Ian muttered to himself.

Nothing had changed inside the Tahoe Saloon. In fact, it struck Ian that even the faces hadn't changed. He was instantly recognized and men nodded to him but no one showed much enthusiasm. Ian went over to the bar.

"Hello, Lars. How's business these days?"

"What are you doin' up here?"

Ian smiled disarmingly. "Oh, I just thought I'd come back to see old friends like you."

"Cut the shit, Ian." Lars filled a mug with beer and shoved it at Ian. "Why don't you have a short drink and move on out of here? I don't want any trouble."

Ian feigned surprise. "Why, Lars! What kind of trouble do you think I'd get into? I never caused any trouble in here before, did I?"

Lars was a stringy old man with a shock of white hair and a bristly white mustache. His face was red, burnt by too many years of sun, and his hands were enormous. "You go away! Helena has chosen a husband. You leave her alone this time."

Ian sipped at the beer. He smiled at the old man's agitation. "You know something? I always thought that I'd be the one to marry Helena. I kind of find that thought a hard one to shake."

"Finish your beer and leave," the man said in a voice that shook with anger.

Ian pretended not to hear. "Why, Helena and I just always seemed to fit together like a hand and a glove. Real tight, you know?"

"I told you. She's got a man!"

"Yeah," Ian said, "I heard about that. Old Joe Bean says she's going to marry Bert Travis. What a shame. He's a damn clod! Probably can't even read or write his own name."

Lars slammed a fist down on his bar so hard that all conversation in the saloon died. "Travis is a *good* man! He'll take care of my daughter."

"I'd take care of her too, Lars. Settle down now. All I want to do is to tell your daughter good-bye and wish her luck and happiness."

"No!"

Ian's smile slipped. "Where is she? In her room upstairs? I mean to see her one last time."

Ian started for the back door but a table of four loggers came to their feet and blocked his path.

One of them, a tall, heavyset man said, "Bert Travis is our friend. I think you'd just better turn around and walk back out the door, Ian. You ain't welcome here anymore."

Ian studied their tough, determined faces. One on one, he wouldn't have been afraid, but he sure wouldn't stand any chance of whipping the four of them. They were brawlers. Men who'd take three punches to land one haymaker.

Ian shrugged and stepped back. "Seems to me like you boys are buying into something that isn't any of your business."

"We're making it our business."

"In that case," Ian said, swinging his arm up and feeling the derringer slap into the palm of his hand, "which one wants to be the first to die?"

The four were caught totally unprepared. Now, they stared at the evil-looking two-shot derringer and it was clear that they were suddenly gripped by fear.

"Which one?" Ian whispered. He shoved the derringer into the heavyset man's face. "You want your brains to decorate the wall? Huh?"

The man went pale with terror. "No!"

"Then sit the hell down and don't get into trouble that is none of your affair."

The four men sat and Ian moved through the back door of the saloon. He climbed a flight of dim stairs that he'd traveled many a dark night and opened the door.

"Hello there," he said, sweeping off his hat. "Helena, honey, it's good to see you again."

She had been reading a magazine and was dressed in a thin and very sexy blue wrapper. At his entrance, she'd spilled the magazine across her large breasts.

"What are you doing in here?"

Ian shrugged and smiled. "Come on, honey," he said, moving to the bed, "you know what I've always come back for."

Ian started to unbutton the gun on his hip.

"Oh, no you don't!" Helena cried. "I'm engaged!"

"Well, engagements are sometimes broken," Ian said, taking off his six-gun and draping it over a bedpost, then slipping out of his coat to reveal the hideout derringer strapped to his arm and upper body.

She stared at him. "You haven't changed anything, have you? Still wearing that derringer."

"And using it," he said, grabbing the magazine and tossing it aside before sitting down next to her. "So, what's this I hear about an engagement to Bert Travis?"

"He loves me!" she said in anger. "And he treats me good. Better'n you ever did!"

Ian's long, slender fingers untied the little silk bow at the front of her nightgown. "I find that very, very hard to believe," he whispered, as his hand reached under her wrapper to caress one of her large breasts.

Helena's mouth opened and even formed a protest, but it was never released. "You're a devil," she panted.

Ian chuckled and bent over her. His mouth took Helena's breast and played with her nipple using the tip of his tongue.

"Stop it," she pleaded weakly. "I'm going to marry Bert!"

"The hell you are," he said, sitting up and beginning to tear off his clothes.

"Please go away," she begged.

THE DEADLY DERRINGER

"Take it off."

Helena swallowed noisily and did as he ordered. When she was completely undressed, Ian chuckled low in his throat. "You get your door lock fixed since I was here the last time?"

"No."

"Figures," he said with contempt. "With Bert Travis, you wouldn't need a lock on your door. He's probably too dumb to know what to do with a body like yours."

"Go away," she breathed.

"Uh-uh," he replied, pushing her silken thighs wide apart and then climbing onto her.

"Oh, Ian!" she moaned as he began to move over her. "I hate you for this!"

He laughed. "I'm going to marry you myself," he said. "I'm going to do it this time for sure."

Helena sobbed and locked her strong legs around his waist. Tears trickled out of the corners of her eyes but her mouth formed a circle of joy.

"Oh, darling!" she cried, feeling her own body begin to shake. "I still love you!"

Ian filled her with his seed. He didn't love her, but he was tired of being alone and on the run.

TWENTY-THREE

"Well," Clint said, pointing down to the lake, "there it is."

"Yeah," Abe Timber grunted, very unimpressed, "but there's dozens of little towns and settlements all around it. Gonna be hard to find Ian Palmer."

"No, it won't," Clint said. "A man like that Palmer will always attract attention. All we have to do is look very closely wherever high-stakes poker is played. Sooner or later, Ian will be drawn to it like a moth to the flame."

Josh studied the lake for several minutes and then he said, "That's the clearest water I ever saw. You can even see the big rocks underneath the surface from way up here."

"It's good fishing but mighty cold swimming," Clint said. "I can tell you that for a fact."

The Gunsmith waited until their horses had recovered their wind. The elevation up here was considerably higher than their horses were accustomed to, and breathing on the steep climb had been difficult.

"Let's start down at this south end," he said, "and then we'll work our way around on the Nevada side and up to the top. If we don't find him on this side, we'll cover the California side next."

Josh and Abe Timber nodded and followed the Gunsmith down into the piney basin where a rutted old logging road circled the lake. The road was well used by freight wagons, many of them carrying timber over to the Carson Valley and on up to the Comstock Lode.

"Damn busy place," Abe grunted after they were forced to swing off the road for about the hundredth time in order to accommodate a pair of huge logging wagons.

Clint gazed out across the lake. He could see at least ten steamboats, most of which were dragging armadas of logs across the water to various sawmills along the shore. Up on the California side, he was saddened to observe about a hundred acres of totally logged-off mountainside.

"I hope that they don't strip everything off these slopes," he said.

"Why shouldn't they?" Abe growled.

"Because it'd look like hell in the first place. And in the second place, it'd leave nothing to hold the soil in the spring when the snow melts. Tons of mud would come washing down these steep slopes and end up in the lake. It'd kill the fish and ruin it, maybe forever."

"Men got to work to eat," Abe said. "There's more lakes."

"Not like this one," Clint snapped as they fell into silence and rode on.

The first saloon they visited was called Big Lil's Place and even though they didn't find Ian Palmer, they bought large bowls of spicy Mexican chili with plenty of hot cornbread on the side for two bits each.

Abe Timber wiped his mouth with the back of his hand and said, "The man who owns this place said he'd put our horses up for the night and grain them for a dollar."

"I'd rather ride on," Clint replied. "We've still got about two hours of daylight. We can get clear around

THE DEADLY DERRINGER 179

the south end of this lake before we camp."

Abe wasn't in favor of riding on. Their horses had really had to hump to climb up the eastern slope of the Sierras and they were tired. Abe was pretty tired himself, being unused to riding all day.

But Clint was determined to press on a few more miles and so they did, stopping at several more saloons until it was nearly dusk and Abe was about to mutiny.

"All right, old fella," Clint said, "just up ahead is the Tahoe Saloon. I know the man who owns it. His name is Lars Andersen and he's honest. Got a daughter that can bake the best apple pie you ever tasted. We'll stop here for the night."

"About time," Abe growled. "Gonna ride these poor horses down to nothin' but skin and bone if we don't slow up some."

Clint glanced over at Josh and winked. Josh winked back.

When they tied their horses up outside the saloon, they went inside to see about getting them a corral and some grain. Lars was tending the bar just the same as always and but there was an uncharacteristic scowl on his lean old face.

"Lars, how you been?"

The big Swede looked up and, recognizing an old friend, managed a thin smile and extended his still-powerful hand to take Clint's in a crushing grip. "Clint Adams. Good to see you again. How long has it been since you passed through?"

"About three years. You married off that handsome blond daughter of yours yet?" Clint asked, thinking about the apple pie.

At the mention of his daughter, Lars reached for a glass of beer and downed it in a shuddering gulp.

"What's the matter?" Clint asked with concern. "Is she all right?"

"No, dammit! She's got all the sense of a bitch in heat!"

Clint frowned. Helena had always been the apple of her father's eye. She was sweet and fun loving. "What does that mean?"

"It means she was betrothed to a good man and she went to bed with and then chose to marry a real bad one!"

"That happens," Clint said. "I guess there's not much a man can do about it. Helena is a full-grown woman. You can't make her marry a man she doesn't love."

Lars growled something unintelligible and said, "What'll you have to drink?"

"Whiskey," Abe told him.

"I'll have the same," Clint said. "And our young friend here will have milk."

"No milk," Lars grunted. "Water or coffee."

"Coffee," Josh said, looking around at the loud and colorful logging men who patronized the Tahoe Saloon.

When their drinks came, Clint made arrangements to put their horses up for the night in Lars's corral. They would be grained and fed cut meadow grass.

"You can sleep in my hay barn or walk down the street about a quarter mile to a cabin where they'll feed and put you up for a dollar."

"We'll do that," Clint said. "By the way, we're looking for a gambling man. He wears a hideout derringer on some kind of spring-loaded device up his sleeve. He's a real bad one. He's shot and killed several men."

Lars had been wiping his polished counter with a dirty rag but now he stopped and stared. "What is this man's name?"

THE DEADLY DERRINGER   181

"Ian Palmer. He's wanted for murder. He'll hang or go down under my gun. I don't much care which."

Lars beamed. "Is that a fact?"

"It's not something I'd kid about," Clint said. "You ever see or hear of him?"

"Yeah," Lars said, his eyes dancing with happiness.

"Really?"

"Yeah! And he's right upstairs in my daughter's room!"

It was the Gunsmith's turn for a big surprise. "Are you sure?"

Lars nodded his head. "He's the one that has ruined my poor Helena. Kill him, Clint. Shoot his balls off and then his . . ."

Clint didn't hear the rest. He was rushing toward the back door of the saloon and up the steps where Lars had once taken him to share a private drink without the distraction of customers.

Clint drew his gun and mounted the stairs quietly. Josh and Abe had followed him and were crowding the bottom of the stairs.

"Abe, you go outside and wait in the back in case he tries to run," Clint hissed. "Josh, you wait down here in case he gets past me."

Josh nodded and Abe vanished. Clint gave the old liveryman about two minutes before he continued up the stairs and put his hand on the door handle. It was probably going to be locked, but he'd shoot it off and burst inside without losing more than a second or two.

To Clint's amazement, the handle turned and so, with a violent shove, he charged inside the room and caught Ian Palmer and Helena asleep.

"Wake up!"

They both came awake fast and when Palmer saw the Gunsmith, he lunged for his six-gun hanging on the bedpost. Clint jumped forward and slammed the barrel of his Colt down across the gambler's forearm.

Palmer howled in pain. Helena cried out and pulled the sheets up to her chin. "Get out of here! Leave us alone!"

Clint was sorry for the girl, but she'd made her own bed and this trouble went a long way beyond modesty and manners.

"Get dressed, Palmer. You've got an appointment with a hanging judge in Virginia City."

"I should have put another bullet in you!" the gambler said.

"Yeah," Clint said, "you should have and you didn't. But it's a mistake that you won't live long to regret."

Palmer climbed out of bed stark naked. He reached for his pants but Clint jumped forward. "Hold on, I mean to check your pockets first."

He checked the pockets and found nothing but a jackknife and less than a dollar's worth of change. "Where is it?"

"What?"

"The contraption that slaps that derringer into your hand!"

"Over there on the chair under my coat," Ian said.

Clint went over to the chair and lifted the coat. What he saw was an odd device with wire pulleys and springs and a little holster. The derringer was missing.

"Looking for this?"

Clint swung around just in time to see the derringer materialize in Ian's fist. In a terrible flashback, he finally remembered how big that little gun looked as it opened fire on him from nearly point-blank range.

Clint jumped sideways and the derringer barked once, twice. The Gunsmith rolled on the floor, firing. Helena screamed even louder when Ian staggered with one of Clint's bullets in his shoulder. Ian lunged for the open window.

"Stop!" Clint shouted.

But Ian wasn't stopping. With one leg out and one leg in, he was going to jump and before Clint could squeeze off a warning shot, old Abe Timber fired twice from down in the alley. One bullet shattered the window but the second hit Ian in the stomach and exited through his back, opening a bloody hole just below his ribs. For a moment, Ian tottered on the sill, and then he rolled forward and disappeared.

Helena screamed and ran to the window. Clint picked himself up and followed her to look down at the still, white body plastered to the earth below.

"I had to kill him," Abe Timber shouted up to them. "I couldn't let him get away stark naked like that, now could I?"

"No," Clint said. "You did just fine."

The old man grinned.

"What am I going to do now?" Helena sobbed hysterically.

Clint had no interest in comforting her as she stood beside the window with her hands covering her face and tears leaking between her fingers.

"I don't know," he said. "But if it's any consolation to you, a lot of other good women fell hard over that man. Every damned one of them ended up cussing his name."

The Gunsmith turned and went back to the door. Lars and Josh came rushing upstairs. Clint let Lars on through because his daughter needed her father.

"Not you, though," Clint said, grabbing Josh by the arm and turning him around to start him back down the stairs. "There's nothing you need to see up there."

"I already saw her naked," Josh said. "Anyway, where are we going now?"

Clint stood at the head of the dim stair landing and listened to the old man try to console his foolish daughter.

"We're going down to Virginia City," he said finally. "I want you to meet Miss Joanna Rogers."

"What for?"

"She needs a friend. I think you and her would hit it off together just fine."

"She's too old for me!"

"I said a friend," Clint repeated. "Like the lady we're leaving behind up here, Miss Rogers isn't even thinking about another lover."

Josh looked at the Gunsmith with a question in his eyes but Clint was not in the mood to furnish an answer. The boy would find out soon enough about loving women. But first, maybe he needed to see that their hearts could also be broken and, in knowing, he'd be a better man.

Clint hoped so. The last thing the world needed was another sweet-talking four-flusher like Ian Palmer.

Watch for

THE STAGECOACH KILLERS

122nd novel in the exciting GUNSMITH series from Jove

Coming in February!

If you enjoyed this book, subscribe now and get...

TWO FREE

A $7.00 VALUE—

If you would like to read more of the very best, most exciting, adventurous, action-packed Westerns being published today, you'll want to subscribe to True Value's Western Home Subscription Service.

Each month the editors of True Value will select the 6 very best Westerns from America's leading publishers for special readers like you. You'll be able to preview these new titles as soon as they are published, *FREE* for ten days with no obligation!

TWO FREE BOOKS

When you subscribe, we'll send you your first month's shipment of the newest and best 6 Westerns for you to preview. With your first shipment, two of these books will be yours as our introductory gift to you absolutely *FREE* (a $7.00 value), regardless of what you decide to do. If you like them, as much as we think you will, keep all six books but pay for just 4 at the low subscriber rate of just $2.75 each. If you decide to return them, keep 2 of the titles as our gift. No obligation.

Special Subscriber Savings

When you become a True Value subscriber you'll save money several ways. First, all regular monthly selections will be billed at the low subscriber price of just $2.75 each. That's at least a savings of $4.50 each month below the publishers price. Second, there is never any shipping, handling or other hidden charges—*Free home delivery*. What's more there is no minimum number of books you must buy, you may return any selection for full credit and you can cancel your subscription at any time. A TRUE VALUE!

A special offer for people who enjoy reading the best Westerns published today.

WESTERNS!

NO OBLIGATION

Mail the coupon below

To start your subscription and receive 2 FREE WESTERNS, fill out the coupon below and mail it today. We'll send your first shipment which includes 2 FREE BOOKS as soon as we receive it.

Mail To: **True Value Home Subscription Services, Inc. P.O. Box 5235
120 Brighton Road, Clifton, New Jersey 07015-5235**

YES! I want to start reviewing the very best Westerns being published today. Send me my first shipment of 6 Westerns for me to preview FREE for 10 days. If I decide to keep them, I'll pay for just 4 of the books at the low subscriber price of $2.75 each; a total $11.00 (a $21.00 value). Then each month I'll receive the 6 newest and best Westerns to preview Free for 10 days. If I'm not satisfied I may return them within 10 days and owe nothing. Otherwise I'll be billed at the special low subscriber rate of $2.75 each; a total of $16.50 (at least a $21.00 value) and save $4.50 off the publishers price. There are never any shipping, handling or other hidden charges. I understand I am under no obligation to purchase any number of books and I can cancel my subscription at any time, no questions asked. In any case the 2 FREE books are mine to keep.

Name _____

Street Address _____ Apt. No. _____

City _____ State _____ Zip Code _____

Telephone _____

Signature _____
(if under 18 parent or guardian must sign)

10755

Terms and prices subject to change. Orders subject to acceptance by True Value Home Subscription Services, Inc.

J.R. ROBERTS
THE
GUNSMITH

___THE GUNSMITH #105: HELLDORADO	0-515-10403-5/$2.95
___THE GUNSMITH #106: THE HANGING JUDGE	0-515-10428-0/$2.95
___THE GUNSMITH #107: THE BOUNTY HUNTER	0-515-10447-7/$2.95
___THE GUNSMITH #108: TOMBSTONE AT LITTLE HORN	0-515-10474-4/$2.95
___THE GUNSMITH #109: KILLER'S RACE	0-515-10496-5/$2.95
___THE GUNSMITH #110: WYOMING RANGE WAR	0-515-10514-7/$2.95
___THE GUNSMITH #111: GRAND CANYON GOLD	0-515-10528-7/$2.95
___THE GUNSMITH #112: GUNS DON'T ARGUE	0-515-10548-1/$2.95
___THE GUNSMITH #113: ST. LOUIS SHOWDOWN	0-515-10572-4/$2.95
___THE GUNSMITH #114: FRONTIER JUSTICE	0-515-10599-6/$2.95
___THE GUNSMITH #115: GAME OF DEATH	0-515-10615-1/$3.50
___THE GUNSMITH #116: THE OREGON STRANGLER	0-515-10651-8/$3.50
___THE GUNSMITH #117: BLOOD BROTHERS	0-515-10671-2/$3.50
___THE GUNSMITH #118: SCARLET FURY	0-515-10691-7/$3.50
___THE GUNSMITH #119: ARIZONA AMBUSH	0-515-10710-7/$3.50
___THE GUNSMITH #120: THE VENGEANCE TRAIL	0-515-10735-2/$3.50

For Visa, MasterCard and American Express orders ($10 minimum) call: 1-800-631-8571

Check book(s). Fill out coupon. Send to:
BERKLEY PUBLISHING GROUP
390 Murray Hill Pkwy., Dept. B
East Rutherford, NJ 07073

NAME _____
ADDRESS _____
CITY _____
STATE_____ ZIP _____

PLEASE ALLOW 6 WEEKS FOR DELIVERY.
PRICES ARE SUBJECT TO CHANGE WITHOUT NOTICE.

POSTAGE AND HANDLING:
$1.50 for one book, 50¢ for each additional. Do not exceed $4.50.

BOOK TOTAL $____
POSTAGE & HANDLING $____
APPLICABLE SALES TAX $____
(CA, NJ, NY, PA)
TOTAL AMOUNT DUE $____
PAYABLE IN US FUNDS.
(No cash orders accepted.)

206c